AWAKEN THE DAUGHTER

The Dawning of Superheroes Book 1

JEREMY FLAGG

Cover Art by
SEAN CARLSON

For those never stop getting up.

Children of Nostradamus Universe

The Dawning of Superheroes

Awaken the Daughter

Anoint the Daughter

Ascend the Daughter

The Night Quartet

Nighthawks

Night Shadows

Night Legions

Night Covenants

The Night Quartet Prequel

Morning Sun

Join the Adventure

For More Children of Nostradamus Visit
www.childrenofnostradamus.com

Chapter One

Cowardice saturated the air. Notes of ego and narcissism mixed with an undercurrent of false bravado. From one man, perhaps two, it might have hidden under the stench of chain-smoking and missing ventilation. There was more than that. It drifted off every man this side of the bar.

They stared.

I didn't need to listen. They whispered, gossiping like a room full of old maids. I violated their sanctuary. At best, they questioned if I entered by accident. At worst, they scanned my body, staring at my breasts, imagining they had a chance of bedding me. How dare a woman come to their drinking establishment to drown her sorrows?

A bear-sized man came up from behind the bar. Shaking his head, he wagged his thick finger to emphasize his disapproval. "No, not again, 'Nore."

I ignored his plea and used my foot to nudge the stool away from the counter. I regretted it the moment I sat down. The shiny lacquer on the top of the stool had transformed into a tacky puddle. Harry attempted to save a nickel by not hiring somebody to clean the surfaces, but he needed help. My forearms rested against the bar, and I waited for him to come to his senses and offer me a drink.

Much like my butt, the counter was sticky, and the layers of filth threatened to stick to the underside of my forearms.

"C'mon, Harry." It was a matter-of-fact statement. There is no flirting to get my way, no batting eyelashes like a youthful harlot. Our game wasn't romantic, more like a battle of circumstance. After he returned from the war with his wooden leg, I behaved. A month later, his grace period had ended. I wanted a drink, and I'd be damned if I left sober.

"I can pour it myself. Quality Scotch is under the counter, right?"

We locked eyes, and the displeasure on his face came with a sneer. He didn't want me there. Not because he feared trading witty banter, but because he was aware of the type of men frequenting his establishment. His protectiveness was both irksome and endearing. It would be far more charming once I drained two fingers of Scotch.

There weren't many bottles on the shelves. With the war raging overseas, few patrons filled the bar and with money tight, he barely maintained an inventory like he once had. An area behind the bar held a wide mirror meant to make the space appear larger. More than one set of eyes lingered on my backside, a slight upturn of the lips. I would have turned and addressed them in a less than lady-like manner if it wouldn't have driven the few remaining patrons from the pub. Harry sensed my bubbling displeasure.

"How many times do I have to ask, 'Nore? They just want to drink in peace and quiet."

The emotion slid from my face as I turned around, eyeing the two gentlemen determined to bore holes through the back of my head. One of the men raised the newspaper, hiding his eyes, but the other gave me a slight nod. The worst kind of pervert is the one aware of his sleaziness. My eyes rolled back, another of those less than lady-like traits I was being told I needed to correct.

"Harry," I turned and smiled. "I've been coming to the bar longer than any of these men."

He leaned forward. A slight grimace flashed across his face as his forearms touch the counter. The scar just right of his nose played hide and seek in his laugh lines. I stifled a chuckle. Had Harry been twenty years younger, he would have been a dashing man. He had never grown out of his boyish charms. They were barely buried beneath the horror of survivor's guilt.

"That's not the same thing."

I pointed at the stool to my side. "I believe that's where he'd sit? By now, he'd have been on what? Drink four?" The guilt grew thicker. "You'd call me to come get him. Those times I went out in the middle of the night to escort him home. Each time thinking, I wouldn't have to do this if Harry would just..."

Harry reached under the counter to produce a tumbler glass. It landed in front of me with a bang. I won. To be fair, I almost felt guilty taking advantage of him. Almost.

"Let's be clear on one thing," Harry poured the drink. "Frank's a grown man capable of his own decisions. You should see that. That thing he does at the gym, doesn't that say he takes ownership?"

More than once, a phone call from Harry had startled me awake. Frank had found himself on the wrong end of the bottle, and instead of going home to sleep it off like a proper drunk, he'd pick fights. Nobody worried about Frank, in fact, Harry feared Frank might beat the living daylights out of another man in the bar.

The whiskey warmed my stomach while it burned my throat. For somebody my size, the first glass would normally be enough to leave them haggard. The amber liquid and I had an abusive relationship that would never end in divorce.

I turned to my left to see a ghost leering at me. With a drink in hand, the ghost of the sleazy patron looked me over from head to toe. Every bone in my body screamed that this man was a predator. Harry went on about how he appreciated me watching out for Frank. His voice came across as distant as I fixated on this specter. His hand reached out, resting atop mine like I was the recipient of a childhood crush.

A ghost separated from my physical self and its transparent limb grabbed the man by the back of the neck and slammed his face onto the bar. The image reset and the ghost blinked out of existence.

"Are you having a spell, 'Nore? Dammit, I knew you shouldn't be drinking."

Frank described the curse as "losing time" to anybody who witnessed the extended periods I stared into space. Every acquaintance experienced my spells. I'd stop speaking mid-sentence or slow until I drifted off. Sometimes they'd pass without notice, other times, I'd go minutes before something dragged me from these nightmares. But Harry was wrong. Booze wasn't the cause, it was the cure.

Spells. They weren't spells, nor daydreams, nor girlish wonderings. Since childhood, demons had plagued me. They became less terrifying as an adult, now reduced to mere ghosts. They'd show me things, things that hadn't happened yet. Despite knowing the future, I remained unable to alter the course of events. They were prophets of false hopes. These ghosts never lied.

"Hello, beautiful."

The sleazy man leaned onto the counter, feigning sincerity. He wasted no time, his hand reaching for mine. The booze made his advances tolerable and bolstered my confidence enough to challenge fate. I resisted the desire to grab him by the head and smash his face against the bar. The ghosts showed me the future, an inevitable path I—

His fingers brushed my leg, his fingertips attempting to slip under my dress. His actions and his demeanor were far from matching. My hand shot out, grabbing the back of his head. Before he knew what was happening, his head bounced off the bar. He grunted his disapproval at my display of feminism. I tightened my grip as I debated repeating the action.

Harry barked at the men as they got to their feet. They only showed solidarity when they believed themselves capable of winning a fight. Cowards. I would have been glad to get into a tumble and show them my right hook.

"Eleanor Bouvier!"

Susan Lee's voice was out of place in this establishment. The bar's rough and dingy interior couldn't diminish her proper and innocent sensibilities. It was the reason I loved and hated the woman. The man's greasy hair was still in my grip when I looked over my shoulder, she was dressed just as I imagined, in a modest dress the color of watered-down whiskey.

"Jesus," Harry tolerated me, but he wouldn't tolerate another broad in his bar. "Susan Lee, take her out of here before I have to call Frank."

I tightened my fist, and the sleazeball let out a slight squeal. I squeezed until I was certain I had torn his scalp. Leaning in close, inches away from his face I whispered, "Remember this next time you do something gross, creep."

"'Nore."

"I'll be checking in on you."

"'Nore!"

I released the man and raised my hands in the air as a sign of peace. "I'll let Frank know you say hello." And with that, I took Susan Lee by the arm and we skedaddled from the bar.

"I can't believe you did that."

I sat at the kitchen table, mulling over the man's intentions. Susan Lee pulled the glass off the lamp and fished for one of the tiny slivers of wood in the matchbox. With a strike, the room lit up briefly before returning to its near dark state. Once the wick caught on fire, the room glowed a soft orange, accenting the hideous yellow paint covering the walls.

Susan Lee kept quiet the entire trek to our apartment. The pull of her arm and the pace of her walk gave away the subtle notes of anger. Based on her clothes, she had been at her Bible group. She often asked me to attend, but I didn't have the heart to tell her there was no God, and if I was wrong, the man upstairs was a real jerk.

"He put his hands on me first."

"Eleanor..."

I predicted the words before she said them. We had almost nothing in common. She was a modest, God-fearing woman who worked as a nurse at the local hospital. I, on the other hand, had a knack for playing the numbers when gambling. We were as similar to oil and vinegar, and despite that, our friendship started the day we met.

"You're twenty-five, you're not a petulant girl. That's not how a lady acts."

Those words. A lady. Other than my anatomy, I wasn't even close to her definition of a proper woman. She corrected my manners, scowled when I swore, and more than once, she offered me a spot in her prayer group. She never said it outright, but I knew she prayed for my troubled soul. I found her friendly nature to be naïve, but admired how she saw the world as a magical place. But that wasn't why I allowed her a room at my "father's" apartment.

Susan Lee removed her favorite church hat, using it as a bowl to collect the many bobby pins fixing her hair in place. She pulled off each of her white gloves, laying them neatly on the table. Sitting in the vacant chair next to mine, she rested a hand on my thigh, a comforting gesture. Susan Lee observed early in our friendship how I flinched at being touched. I'm sure she created a narrative that involved me being abused by my parents to explain why I avoided physical contact. I never explained the truth to her in an effort to keep this perfect companionship.

When her skin made contact with my leg, it didn't agitate the ghosts. They never emerged when Susan Lee violated my personal space.

"I don't understand why you go looking for trouble, and *there* of all places."

How did I convey this secret to Susan Lee? This woman believed God had a plan for each of us, that somewhere between the first and third drink, ghosts I had seen my entire life, left me alone? I gave her hand a slight squeeze with my own. She meant well. Her heart was in the right place. My demons weren't meant for her, not yet.

"I have issues." It wasn't a lie.

"I don't want to see something awful happen to you. Even if you refuse to wear makeup and insist on wearing slacks all the time, you're still a pretty woman. Those men are capable of horrible things." She leaned in close, as if she didn't want the Lord to hear her words. "They're monsters. You're just asking for trouble."

Yes, me, a slender woman with muscles unseen through my blouse was the one who should be fearful. This was one of the many times I wanted to reveal my secret, to confess that the devil spoke to me. I could tell her about a revolution, where women were equals. It wasn't all roses and sunshine, but after a battle of the sexes, we emerged victorious. Eventually, they respected us for more than our ability to make dinner and bare children.

"Have you been smoking?" I couldn't tell her about the future. To tell the truth, I wasn't sure when it happened. Instead, I swung the conversation to a place that even Susan Lee shied away from.

"Me? I'm not one of *those* girls."

"Oh, good." Susan Lee was a horrible liar. "I'll say a prayer for you, none the less." She didn't know if she should smile at my admitting some connection to God or scared that I invoked His name regarding her fib.

We all had our vices. Susan Lee fractured her good-girl image once in a while, hanging out her window on the fire escape to sneak a fag. I found it humanizing, and I was glad that even my goodie-two-shoes roommate gave in to temptations. If she discovered my vices, I feared she would faint.

"I think it's time for bed. I'm working at the hospital tomorrow and then volunteering to roll bandages."

"You're a wonderful woman, Susan Lee. You inspire me."

She smiled. The compliment was genuine. She reminded me to be a better person, regardless of the unfair hand life had dealt me.

"Those poor men, they need our support."

She stood, picking up the oil lamp by the base. "If you have time tomorrow, join me and the other women. It would be good for you to socialize with some civilized individuals."

"You never know. I might do just that."

Susan Lee scooped up her hat and gloves and retired to her bedroom. The moment I shut the door to my room, she'd hang out the window like a call girl. She'd ease her guilt with prayers and reading verses of the Bible in hushed whispers.

Early June in the city meant the sun shined hot enough to scramble an egg on the sidewalk and when it set, the air turned chilly, requiring a housecoat. Hours passed before I admitted I needed to crack the window. I couldn't recall the last time I slept through the night. More often than not, I laid in bed staring at the chips of paint on the ceiling threatening to tear themselves free.

Only a short time before the sun rose, New York already stirred.

The first gust of cool air pushing into my room reminded me of the farm from a previous life. With a deep breath, the smell of the city brushed aside the past and revealed the scent of asphalt and sadness.

It had taken me years to fall in love with New York. Frank had brought me here for a fresh start, to put as much mental and physical distance between me and my childhood. More people meant more ghosts, more demons chasing me in the streets. After a while, they looked like every other New Yorker, and they became permanent residents only I saw.

I was sprawled out in bed on top of the blankets. Staring at the ceiling, I closed my eyes and hoped sleep greeted me quickly. Alone in the darkness, I could identify something similar to the ghost in the bar. Unlike the transparent man, these visions are quick flashes of events somewhere in a distant future.

An elderly woman held a compact pistol. Another woman's mouth was moving in a manner that suggested she was shouting, but I couldn't hear the words. The images distorted, blinking in and out of sight. A second lady smiled as two men rushed into the room.

The first woman was on the floor, her weapon a few feet from her hand. A red blotch forming on the exterior of her powder-blue jacket. I could see her face clearly and it reminded me of my mother. For a moment I wondered if it might be Momma, and then the realization jolted me upright in bed.

No, not Momma. Me.

Chapter Two

Frank is my Godfather, or at least that's what I tell Susan Lee. He served with my father, and after I was orphaned, he rescued me. For a while he worked as a firefighter, determined to save people. I warned him the roof would collapse when he tried to rescue a toddler from a burning house, but Frank had a code. He'd sacrifice himself if it meant saving another. We took care of each other.

From the outside, the building resembled every other on the block. A series of windows interrupted the three stories of brick on the second and third floors. Like much of New York, the warehouse had gone into disrepair, windows missing panes either from neglect or hooligans.

In this part of the city, few wandered the streets. There were men sitting on a stoop on the other side of the street, their eyes glued to me as I walked. My insistence on wearing trousers often caused confusion when they realized the man they watched had an ample bosom.

The newest wave of propaganda posters were slathered across the brick walls on either side of the gym doors. At least this time, the wretches avoided pasting them over the windows. One had a pilot in a fighter jet looking stoic with the slogan, "You give us fire, we'll give 'em hell." America had become a munitions factory line.

Women stood in rows, preparing the great war machines to stop Hitler from conquering Europe.

The fear tactics in most posters bordered on frightening. The second poster however, elicited pangs of guilt. A lady of leisure wearing red, white, and blue reclined on a sofa. "Wake Up, America, Civilization Calls Every Man, Woman, and Child." While I deemed the men in the bar cowards, I didn't pull my weight, not compared to Susan Lee. At some point, I'd have to discuss this with her and do my civic duty. America needed each of us on some level. Nobody liked a hypocrite.

I pushed through the front door and before it shut, I smelled the sweat. I enjoy a man glistening after a hard day's work, but this was stale, an almost sour scent that made my eyes water. If it wasn't for the dozen attractive men making use of Frank's gym, I'd have thrown his lunch at him and bailed before I took another breath.

The space was massive. It felt too big for those working out. There were weights along the wall under the windows to my right and a few punching bags being beaten relentlessly by several men. A few racks to my left held free weights and medicine balls. At the far end of the gym was the ring—Frank's pride and joy. He believed every argument could be settled with a boxing match. More than once we carried an entire conversation with our fists. What happened in the ring stayed there. I might scoff at his philosophy, but our disagreements never spilled over the ropes.

"Eleanor," Nicholas waved. He wiped the sweat off his forehead with a towel before leaning back on a bench to resume his weightlifting.

"I want to see that bar touching your chest." The regulars had grown accustomed to me in their space. Once you beat a man in the ring, they can either scurry away with their tails tucked between their legs or admit I belonged.

"Hi, honey," winked Vincent by the punching bag.

"Keep those wrists straight."

I knew everybody in the room. Most were ex-military or retired from firefighting. Unlike the men in Harry's bar, these were heroes. Each had given a bit of themselves to make the world a better place.

Nicholas couldn't see, and Vincent was prone to seizures. They were regulars at Frank's gym.

Unable to remain in the army, Frank fulfilled his mission to do good by joining the New York Fire Department. When that dream crumbled, he turned to the building inherited from his father. He gave all of himself to those in need. Eventually it took the form of this gym. Here, he continued his mission by helping wounded vets.

Frank was the best of what men hoped to become. He wasn't perfect by any stretch. He had spent years in an abusive relationship with bourbon. The man had a knack for scolding me for my behavior, and we frequently gave each other looks that cleared a room. I had never referred to him as my father, but I believed my dad and Frank were cut from the same cloth.

"Frank, I brought your lunch."

Frank spotted a neg—a black man lifting weights sitting in a wheelchair. Both of his pant legs were folded under and pinned. I didn't have to ask to know he had somehow lost his limbs during the war. Since America got involved, more and more men returned broken. Each went through the process: anger, grief, sorrow, depression. The lucky ones eventually snapped out of it and realized it was better than returning in a body bag. Those that didn't, they found their way into one. Frank was the barrier between them and that untimely end.

"Two more, don't quit on me." Frank's hands rested on the man's elbows as he lifted a weight in each hand above his head. The man struggled, his arms shaky.

"I can't," he growled.

"Nobody likes a quitter," I said.

The man stared me in the eye as he lowered the weights to ear level. His growl grew louder as his hands shot upward. Frank grabbed the bar before the man's arms gave out. I winked at the soldier, and he almost snorted, the edge of lip pulling into a smile.

"Michael, meet Eleanor. Michael is our newest member."

I extended my hand to the man. He hesitated before reaching out and giving it a slight shake.

When I tried to sleep, I frequently saw flashes of a distant future. I didn't know when they happened, but considering the world I lived in now, I had to assume it was hundreds of years away. But someday, our black brothers and sisters united. Eventually they, along with women stood as equals. Until that glorious day, I did my best to foster progression.

"Michael, there are two sandwiches in there. Frank, don't be a pig. Share with the man."

"Eleanor…"

Michael chuckled at Frank's subtle attempt to make me be nice. "Michael knows what I'm saying. For somebody who owns a gym, that belly doesn't seem to go away." With a light rub of his stomach, Frank grimaced, annoyed that I harped on his health.

Frank rolled his eyes as he walked away to put the weights on the rack. Michael kept averting his eyes, darting back and forth to take stock of the other men.

"You ignore them," I said. "Frank has a way of helping anybody back from the war."

"Eleanor, is he bothering you?" My teeth ground from the sound of Tony's racist ego.

Michael dropped his gaze. He gripped the wheels of his chair, prepared to speed away from the confrontation. I slipped my foot under the wheel to prevent him from leaving. Dropping the bag of food in Michael's lap, I straightened my back, ready to deal with the biggest chucklehead in the room.

A ghost emerged from Michael and I wasn't sure if I was in danger. Michael's ghost was looking over my left shoulder, glancing at the arrogant fool. I didn't just dislike Tony—I loathed the man and his absolute disregard for anybody other than himself. The caveman needed to be taught a lesson.

I spun on my left foot and my chest bumped against Tony's bare skin. He was over six inches taller than me, but a man's stature had never impressed me. I leaned in until he took a step back.

"Were you addressing my friend here? His name is Michael."

"He's just another colored—"

"Say his name." I drove the tip of my finger into Tony's sweaty chest, hard enough that it'd leave a mark.

"Frank, you need to watch your dame." If he expected an ally in controlling me, he looked to the wrong man.

It was time. I shoved Tony with both hands. I was grumpy from lack of sleep. But more than that, I was exhausted with dealing with jerks who believed themselves better. I was done.

"In the ring," I yelled.

"You don't need to do that," Michael said, "I'll be on my way."

I pointed at Michael. "You, stay." The other hand pointed at Tony. "You, you heard me."

"Frank, she can't be—"

"Does Frank look like my caretaker?" I'll admit, I was overreacting to the idiot's statements. Michael didn't deserve to have his humanity stripped away by this cretin. I should have cursed him up and down and let it be. Tony had lost a toe and used the opportunity to escape the war. Frank tolerated him, part of his peace-keeping mission to help every veteran. I, however, I wanted to pop him in the nose.

Frank shot me a stern glance so often it might as well have been the default expression on his face. He shook his head, disapproving of my act of aggression. The lack of protest was the closest thing I'd get for approval from him. The tension broke as Nicholas yelled across the gym.

"Did she knock the spit out of Tony? Somebody help a blind man."

"She's about to," Vincent laughed.

Tony's honor was on the table as the men in the gym stopped their rehabilitation to see how he would react. He searched the room for allies and found that nobody cheered for him. They didn't care that he was a fellow serviceman; they were prepared to put their money on the angry woman in khaki trousers. Smart men.

"Fine," he stepped to the side and took a bow, gesturing for me to head toward the boxing ring. "After you."

"This will be fun."

"Frank, I'll take it easy on your little lady here."

Lady. I'm not sure anybody had ever referred to me as a lady. Despite Susan Lee's determination to transform me into a civilized young woman, I still managed a questionable reputation. People who've met me call me a daydreamer, odd, or quirky more often than that. The men at the gym tell me I'm one of the "boys" like it's a compliment, as if having a penis is a gift.

No, I'm a woman out of time. For those surrounding the boxing ring, this is the present. They're living their lives now and looking forward to the future. I envy them. Their present is often my past.

Frank lifted the bottom rope of the ring and blocked me with an arm. In the locker room he had fished out gym clothes left behind by a former vet. A men's small shirt hung loose on my chest. I was certain if I moved or ducked too quickly one of my breasts would escape out the side. I'm not modest, but it's hard to beat the snot out of a man when you're baring your breasts.

"You know the rules," he whispered.

"I know. No ghosts."

"No ghosts," he repeated. Frank was the only person alive who knew about the curse. He didn't understand it, but he believed me when I told him I could see things before they happened. It was far-fetched and required faith. Even I sometimes thought I sounded crazy when I spoke about the future.

I climbed onto the boxing ring and rolled under the rope. Tony was already starting to hop around, unaffected by his missing toe. He took swings at a phantom opponent, hoping to intimidate me. I didn't intimidate easily.

"What's happening?" Nicholas asked.

"Eleanor just got in the ring. Tony thinks he looks like a big man," Vincent said.

"He's dead," Nicholas said.

I approached Tony, gloves out, ready to bump fists. He stopped bouncing and walked toward me. The ghosts were stepping out of Tony, three of them, different points in the future. I shook my head, and they dimmed slightly, refusing to go away. His gloves pressed against mine and the next thing I knew pain spread along my jaw as I staggered backward and fell.

"Is he down?"

"Hush, man," Vincent said.

The taste of copper filled my mouth. I spat and could see the blood spray across the mat. I didn't move immediately, instead I ran my tongue over my teeth to make sure they were still in place. The ghosts were there, and if I had paid attention, I'd have seen him take a swing at me.

"Frank, you should tell your girl to stay down."

Frank let out a low growl. Had it been a year ago, he would have jumped into the ring and slammed his bare knuckles into Tony's pretty face. Thankfully, over time, he had let me pick my own battles. He might have been my savior once upon a time, but now, he knew the woman I had become.

"Ghost him," Frank whispered.

If Tony played dirty, I could do the same. I pushed myself up until all my weight rested on my knees and gloves. With my adrenaline pumping, transparent specters already filled the ring. I just needed to ask them to focus on Tony. Frank's specter happily clapped. The win was close, the ghosts never lied.

I made a show of standing, taking my time to rise. I wanted Tony to see me, to see I wasn't going to quit. Eleanor Bouvier could take a punch and rebound. When I turned around, I wiped the blood off my lip with the back of my glove. I'm sure I looked crazy, but that was half the fun, Tony was about to get thwacked.

Several ghosts stepped out of his body. Each depicted a moment yet to transpire, a linear path displaying the actions he'd take. The world slowed as I focused on his upcoming offense. While they were concrete images of the future, fate granted me just enough wiggle room to make slight modifications. I could dodge and land a blow, and if I was lucky, destiny would bend, allowing me to leave, free of injuries.

I moved with a purpose and when the right hook swung out wide. Bending over, the bottom of his arm grazed my spine as it passed harmlessly above. Drawing back my right fist, I jolted upright, striking under his chin. I added a little hop, giving it some extra oomph.

His head slowed until he was suspended in a backward stumble. There was a moment to enjoy my handiwork, to see the spit hovering in the air. The scene resumed as he wiped his face, checking for blood on his glove.

"Bitch," he said.

Tony came at me in a flurry, his ghost only providing a split-second warning. It jabbed and before he caught up, I pulled back. His fist fell short by an inch. I stepped to the side and punched his kidney. His ghost's elbow went wide, trying to play dirty. I ducked. He missed. Leaving himself open, I punched his stomach, hard.

Tony stopped boxing and started fighting. The ghosts predicted it, he grabbed me and spun me about in a chokehold. He expected me to beg for mercy, or to at least tap out. The heel of my shoe slammed down on the top of his foot, enough he loosened his grip. An elbow to the gut and the man buckled over. With a final spin, I used my momentum to clock him to the side of the face, sending him to the mat.

"She knocked the piss out of him," Vincent said.

"Atta girl," Nicholas cheered.

I wanted to drive the toe of my foot into his stomach, maybe stomp on his neck until he stopped moving. I spat on the man as I tore off my gloves. Throwing them on Tony, I didn't need to say another word. His ego looked worse than his face. I had made an enemy, but as I crawled out of the ring and passed Michael, I saw the man's smile. I also discovered a friend.

"Go shower," Frank said.

With all the men at my back, I pulled off my shirt and left it lying on the floor. The cheering came to a halt, and I imagined Frank hung his head at my lack of modesty.

"Stop staring, gentlemen," I yelled as I headed toward the locker room.

The picture of Frank in my locker always resulted in a smile. I can't remember a time he'd worn a tie since my sixteenth birthday. In the photograph he had his arm draped over my shoulder as I scowled at the cameraman. Nearly a decade ago, I didn't want to be near other people. Frank ignored my protests. The image served as a reminder to let others into my life and to cherish marvelous times.

I pulled on a pair of sweatpants and an oversized sweatshirt. I shut my locker and went back to drying my hair. Susan Lee would be aghast when I returned home. She'd have me in curlers and ready to style the next morning. Why she spent so much time pinning her curls into place, I'd never understand. I looked forward to the day when women could put their hair into a ponytail and not get weird looks.

I shoved my towel into my locker and gave the photograph one more look before shutting the door. The hinge resisted, and I tried again, putting my weight into it. While the gym didn't need to be the most glamorous thing, the locker room needed love. Tiles shook loose from the floor and there were breaks in the drywall where an angry man had punched it. As I walked to the open area, equipment littered the hallway. I'd have to let Frank know to bark at the men.

Frank set up folding chairs in a circle. The other vets had left; I'm sure Frank blocked their way into the locker room telling them they could shower at home. Chairs in a circle meant it was Friday and gentlemen would start showing up for alcoholics anonymous.

"You didn't have to fight him," Frank said.

"Tony is a jerk. I wouldn't let him treat Michael like that."

"Your heart is in the right place," He stopped to inspect the circle. He quickly realized he'd made an oval and started adjusting the seats. "How many times have we had this talk. You know things will change for Michael's people. We don't all have the luxury of seeing your utopia."

Frank knew my secret, my curse. He accepted it. When I'd lived with him, the visions woke me in the middle of the night screaming. He'd carry me to the couch to watch over me. I knew he couldn't stop them, but having him in his worn-out chair watching me sleep made a difference.

"You know the ghosts show me these things before they happen. I can't change it. It meant I'd be in the ring with Tony." I lied. I hadn't seen the fight before it happened, but now and then I could use them to avoid an argument. Frank knew I could see the future, just like he was fully aware I couldn't alter what they showed me.

He sighed. That sigh was the reason I didn't tell other people about my curse. If the ghosts revealed themselves, I would know the outcome of every fight, every question, every action. It was hard to have a conversation with somebody in the present when they were part of my past. He empathized with my reality, and he continued to put up with it.

"Frank, do you remember when I used to have those visions?"

He froze with a chair in his hand. The ghosts showed me the immediate future, minor things a few seconds or minutes before they happened. The visions, however, they were more like dreams, glances into a distant timeline. I had predicted the rise of Hitler, years before he came into power. Glimpses revealed the involvement of America in a war unlike any we had seen before. Thankfully, it also told me the date it ended.

"One of *those* visions?"

I nodded.

"Aliens? Maybe this time—"

"I saw myself, dead." The chair dropped. Frank walked through his newly formed circle and wrapped his arms around me. I didn't realize how much seeing my death had shaken me. I was thankful it was far off and hopefully I'd have a wonderful life between now and then. As he squeezed me, I was sixteen again, and he was in the living room standing guard.

I hugged his barrel chest and clutched him tightly. My future was inevitable and there was nothing I could do to change it. Instead of explaining myself and asking for Frank's point of view, my body shook. I buried my face and cried.

Chapter Three

The ghosts were everywhere.

Once upon a time, they terrified me. Their appearance used to mean something horrible would happen. Momma had called them tricks of the devil. I believed they were a punishment, showing me a tragic future and robbing me of the ability to intervene. Now, they have abandoned their bad omen status and showed themselves whenever they needed an audience.

The green here isn't large compared to the splendor of Central Park, but it's big enough to forget about the concrete jungle surrounding three sides. There are fewer people here, most too scared to leave the sidewalks and sprawling streets. It provided a break from the perpetual haunting of phantoms. Each time a ghost stepped out of a youthful woman, I feared an atrocity would unfold. Old habits clung to the present.

"Thanks for coming out, Jonathon was driving me mad." Two young ladies were sitting on a bench next to mine. Both of them were, as Susan Lee would describe, civilized women. They wore fashionable ankle-length dresses and their hair was curled and held in place by dozens of unseen bobby pins. Even the manner in which they sat, legs crossed at the ankles and hands resting on their laps reinforced the etiquette expected of proper women.

"At least Jonathon is home. I haven't heard from William in almost two months." The woman in a red floral print sighed, furrowing her brow as she worried. It was the same story every time they shipped her husband overseas to fight in a barbaric war.

"Do you know what he told me? He wished he could go back. Can you believe that, Cindy? He'd rather be fighting than stay at home watching J.J."

I pulled out a newspaper and opened it. I didn't plan on reading, but sitting there staring off into space would garner attention from the two hens. Being drawn into a conversation was not something I wanted. While I'm sure they were lovely ladies, I couldn't fathom having a sympathetic discussion about the war without commenting on the impending death of Hitler next year.

"Betty, I'm certain that's not what he meant. He's a kind man, he just wants to protect his family." Cindy took Betty's hand in her own. "Your husband cherishes you, and J.J."

Betty let out an exasperated sigh. It took a moment, but she mumbled, "I know." In New York City, there were hundreds, if not thousands of these conversations happening. Speculation about the life and death of fighting husbands occurred everywhere. Everybody knew somebody who received the infamous letter. Every day, the mail arrived and women held their breath, fearful of a single sheet of paper that would declare them a widow.

"William is fine," Betty said. "That man knows how to take care of himself. If I was a betting woman, I'd put my money on him."

She'd lose. The apparitions are there, only transparent specters, until Betty reaches into her clutch to pull out a pack of fags. The ghosts moved quickly, far faster than normal, as the phantoms of the two women walked out of the park. I saw flashes of Betty holding a letter. She clings to the man who delivered it. I can't hear her wailing, but the contortion of her face gives away her grief.

Those flashes are why I avoid people. Momma called me blunt, and Frank said I had a knack for brutal honesty. I'm not sure I could maintain an expressionless facade knowing the woman was about to receive a death note. For me, it's easier to mind my business and let Betty live thinking William was alive.

She reached into her clutch and liberated a single cigarette. Cindy tried to keep a nonchalant disposition, but the shock hit her eyes. Betty was a bit of a rogue. She playfully swatted at Cindy and struck a match, lit the tip and took a deep drag. I can only imagine the hardship of being a model housewife. The woman reminded me why I remained unmarried.

Betty politely offered the cigarette to Cindy. She hesitated a moment too long to have never thought about it. One of her ghosts snatched the slender white tube, and she enjoyed a long drag. I turned my face to hide my smile. Cindy wasn't as prim and proper as she wanted others to think. The ghosts never lied.

"Another one?"

It took a second before I realized Betty wasn't talking to Cindy. I glance sideways at the two women. Betty pointed at me.

"Excuse me?" I didn't have a blasted idea at what she was gesturing.

"Goodness," Cindy said, "what has happened to this city? It's barely safe to be out in the daylight."

I folded the newspaper and caught the headline on the front page, "Man Murdered, Still No Suspects." The residents liked to insist crime never happened in New York City. With every article depicting gruesome photographs from the frontline of the war, it was easy to forget the city had a dark underbelly.

"I heard Martha, her husband owns the deli, you know the one?" Betty started. "She said the young man last week was a regular. She said he was a friendly boy."

The closeness appeared to insult Cindy's sensibilities. "So close to home. These streets just aren't safe."

I didn't give it much thought. I knew it was horrible to think. But, with a war going on and our troops dying by the thousands, a few deaths in a city, known to be dangerous, didn't strike me as a big deal. I gave a slight smile. "You two ladies be careful."

"We can't leave you here," Betty said. "We'll walk home with you."

I should have kept my mouth shut. "Thank you, but I'm—"

"No," Cindy said with a smile, "we insist."

As I brushed off my slacks, both women raised their eyebrows. They were polite enough to keep their misgivings to themselves, but

I had grown accustomed to the wayward judgments of these traditional ladies. I folded the paper under my arm and gave them my best smile.

"I'm Betty, and this is Cindy," she said beaming. When I hesitated, she followed up. "And you are?"

"Eleanor." I harnessed my inner Susan Lee and flashed a smile. I had to remind myself these women were attempting to do a good deed.

Where was a serial killer when you needed one?

The city was dirty. I wasn't only speaking of the streets, but the people too. It might have been because the honorable men were off fighting the war. Those that remained were less than reputable. Betty and Cindy were a rare breed, lovely women who wanted to protect another human.

Standing on the roof of our building gave me a fresh perspective. From here, I couldn't see the individuals littering the streets rushing to get home. As the sun dipped below the horizon, the grandeur of the city unfolded, the tips of the buildings touching the heavens. A breeze chased away the warmth of the day, leaving me hugging myself.

There were no people, no ghosts. If I closed my eyes and dozed, the visions would make themselves known. I kept them open until the tears ran down my cheeks. I didn't want a beautiful, tranquil moment interrupted by some ghastly image of a tragedy I couldn't prevent.

The newspaper article said the victim had his throat slashed with a knife. It only loosely mentioned the other murders. I assumed the writer wanted to avoid hysteria, but for it to sit above the fold during a war, it was obvious there was city-wide concern—seven deaths, and still no suspects.

If I could see events that had yet to happen, I wondered if the ghosts could look in the other direction as well? It had never happened, but we were in uncharted territory. If I couldn't change the future, perhaps the past would give me hints forward? Next time

I saw Frank, I'd have to talk to him about it. He hardly understood women, let alone one haunted by the devil. But, he was the closest thing I had to a mentor.

Below, I heard the window lift as Susan Lee worked her way onto the fire escape. She dug around in her purse and I couldn't help but grin as she lit her cigarette. She put on a mask when she left the house, her clothes, makeup, hair, and even her manners were to appease other people. The woman leaning out the window having a moment to herself, that was the real Susan Lee.

"Psst."

Looking up, she froze. She thought I'd caught her in a lie. I caught her in a truth, but I didn't really care either way. Waving her up, she shook her head. I gestured harder, and she rolled her eyes. She caved and climbed the stairs to the roof.

"Are we even allowed up here?"

"I'd think a wicked girl like you would be all for breaking the rules."

She wasn't amused by my joke, not in the slightest. I held out my hand until she gave me that signature grimace. "If you're going to smoke, share."

I don't smoke. I hated the dreadful things, but I wanted to maintain our relationship. I had to be the bad girl. She pulled the pack from her pocket and handed me one. I dangled it between my lips, pointing to the tip. "Help, please."

Susan Lee struck a match and held it against the end of the cigarette. "What are you doing up here?"

I took a drag and forced my lungs into submission as they shook with an impending cough. Susan Lee pulled out another for herself and lit it with an expert strike of the match.

"It's beautiful," I said as I let out a little cough.

She faced toward the sun, squinting as the last of the light bathed her face. Her shoulders shrugged. "I don't know, it seems kind of cold up here. I mean, they're just a bunch of buildings."

"It's peaceful."

"I quite like the busy of the streets. There's something invigorating about all those people. I try to guess what their lives are like."

I knew what their lives were like. I could see as they hurried home and prepared soup for dinner and how they gathered around the radio with the kids. The very thing Susan Lee loved, I found taxing.

"I come up here sometimes to get away from all of that. It's just me and New York. I feel incredibly small. We live in such an enormous world. I like to guess what's beyond the horizon."

"I know you prefer to avoid people, especially strangers—"

"Betty and Cindy walked me home from the park earlier." The moment I said it, I could see the surprise splashed across Susan Lee's face. She would never have predicted those words coming from my mouth.

"You, the great Eleanor Bouvier, escorted by a pair of ladies?"

I snorted. I deserved her flack. "They were worried about the murders that have been happening. They didn't want me walking home alone."

"I'm sure they needed your safety more than the other way around. And how in the Lord's name did you get that bruise?"

"Boxing at Franks."

"Mm-hmm." She took a long drag of her cigarette, judging my poor choices. "What about the other guy?"

"A broken nose."

"Eleanor Bouvier," she said in a high-pitch voice. It was how she said it that made it clear she'd be saying an extra prayer for me tonight.

"But, Betty and Cindy…"

"Well, since you're feeling social, I have news for you then."

"This can't be good."

"A dashing doctor I work with invited me to a ball tomorrow night. He said it would only be proper if I brought my roommate."

"Did he really?"

"Okay, maybe I asked," Susan Lee smiled. It was hard not to adore that smile. "I said she wouldn't think of turning down such an offer."

"I'm not so—"

"There's a killer out there, Eleanor. You wouldn't want me attending a party alone? I might have one too many glasses of wine. I'd be defenseless."

Susan Lee, the vixen, schooled me. I'm sure the dashing doctor was code for eligible bachelor, but I couldn't turn down her invitation now. She'd trapped me in my self-righteousness. Well played, Susan Lee.

"Fine. It looks like I'm attending a ball."

She flicked the cigarette and clapped her hands like a giddy schoolgirl. I couldn't help but laugh at how much joy she took at watching me squirm. She climbed onto the fire escape and proceeded to her window. Susan Lee proved a formidable foe. With anybody else I would have laughed and brushed it off. But somehow, she'd managed the upper hand and sucked me into being her escort.

"It's formal. I shouldn't have to remind you that requires you in a dress."

"Oh, hell."

Chapter Four

The ghosts didn't wait for bedtime.

In the middle of the night, I woke to an empty room. The spot next to me in bed was empty and cool to the touch. Benjie had escaped after I had fallen asleep. I didn't need to look. He'd be under the blankets with Momma, drooling all over her pretty pillows.

I reached for my nightstand, where Momma always left me a glass of water. I sat up and I took a sip, wetting my dry mouth. When I placed it down, Momma entered the room and headed to our closet while holding the laundry basket against her hip.

"Momma?"

I used the back of my hands to rub my eyes. When I finished, she had vanished into the narrow closet. The room was mostly dark, a slither of moonlight coming in through the curtains Momma had sewn. Leaning forward, I couldn't see out the bedroom door. Momma's late-night routine required further inspection.

Slipping out of bed, I made sure I didn't step on the creaky spots on the floor. I tiptoed to the door, poked my head around the corner to check if she'd headed back to her room. She wasn't in the hallway. From her bedroom, I could hear the Benjie snoring like only a boy could.

"Momma?" I whispered, nervous she'd pop out of the bathroom and scare me.

Nothing.

The closet, I thought. I don't know why she'd be putting clothes away at this hour. The floor whined under my feet as I turned toward the closet. Benjie had made it a game, see who could get to the bed without waking the dragon who lived underneath. I never won.

I prepared for Momma to jump out and yell, 'Gotcha!' The door yanked away from the frame. Our closet connected with the linen closet in the hallway, and I was convinced Momma was playing a late-night game of hide and seek. I squished past the shelves of Benjie's old play clothes. He hated the colors, hand-me-downs from when I was his age.

This was Benjie's favorite hiding spot, nestled between my Sunday dress and the shelf holding the good bathroom towels. I yelped when I looked down and saw my baby brother. He drew his legs up to his chest and tucked his head down to make himself as small as possible.

I rubbed my eyes again, determined to push away the sleepies. It was too dark and I couldn't see the clothes, or the blankets, but I could see him, a bright white ghost of my brother. I leaned back, trying to put distance between me and the whiteish boy. My dress fell off the hanger, and I let out a tiny yelp.

"Benjie?" I asked. The boy's head turned, surprised at something happening in the hallway. He darted forward. I tried to back up, but bumped into shelves. He ran by, no, through. He passed *through* my legs. I squealed, scared that the tiny demon would grasp my feet and drag me to Hell.

"Momma," I yelled.

Running, I knocked over a stack of towels. I hit the door in the hallway, knocking it open. I didn't turn or wait for the image of Benjie to follow me. I ran into Momma's room before jumping on her bed, pulled my legs up quickly, crawling between my mother and brother.

"Momma, it tried to get me."

She shot up in bed, reaching for the rifle that rested next to her bed. "Eleanor Paula Bouvier, what has gotten into you?"

"It got Benjie, that thing got him."

She opened her arms, and I crawled up against her, tucking my legs in tight. Every inch of my body touched hers while my arms clung tightly around her neck. She made shushing noises while gently rocking me.

"It's just an awful dream, Ellie."

I shook my head, my eyes held shut, hoping I wouldn't see the bad thing again. "I saw you with the laundry. Then I went into the closet. Benjie was in there, he was."

"He's right here, Ellie. Quiet down, I'll protect you."

The soft promise of Momma willing to defend me halted my whining. But I wasn't convinced she could stop ghosts. But she had a gun, and that scared away the coyotes. Perhaps it would do the same for a ghost.

"I'm right here. Nobody or nothing will hurt you."

I dozed off, Momma gently rocking back and forth, now and then pushing a loose strand of hair behind my ear. I woke as she rolled me onto the bed, caught between her and Benjie. He barely stirred whenever I jumped onto the bed. He resumed his snoring, funny snorting as he inhaled too quickly.

I stole a glance toward my feet, where I feared the evil thing that looked like Benjie might be waiting. I prepared to scream again, but there was nothing, no white ghost of Momma or my baby brother.

Somebody climbed the last stair, eyeing down the hallway before it turned to the bedroom. The devil wasn't scary, more gloomy than anything. It had been almost six months since I saw Poppa. There he stood with his duffle bag slung over his shoulder. His face lit up, beaming from ear to ear. He dropped the bag, and it evaporated, his arms stretched out, dipping low like when he picked me up. With a step forward, he vanished like dust in a hurricane.

I pulled the blankets tight over my head. I didn't want to see things that weren't there. Poppa had left months ago to protect the world like a real knight. For the first few evenings, after dinner we'd wait on the porch, hoping he'd come home. I almost forgot his smile and his chipped front tooth. It wasn't him. It was the scary thing. I tried to be brave and not cry.

I wiggled my butt over until I wrapped around Benjie. My face buried in the back of his neck. Despite him needing a bath, the warmth of his body made me feel safe. I kept my head slightly under the blankets, not wanting to see another one of *them*, the evil creatures infesting our home.

Demons wandered our house like they called it their own.

Chapter Five

"Did I hear you right? Dress shopping?"

I knew he was only half-joking. If I had explained we would look at guns, or go into a speakeasy, he wouldn't have flinched. Hell, Frank hardly batted an eye if I mentioned an underground fight, but searching for an article of clothing, that stopped him cold on the sidewalk.

His dramatic standstill almost elicited a smile, but I refused to be the victim of his charm. He gave his shoulders a roll, shook his arms, and ended with a clap as if the coach was about to put him in the big game. This man wasn't my father, but he had a knack for it, or at least the awful jokes.

"I would show up to the ball tonight in a suit, but—"

Frank clutched at his chest with one hand while bracing the other against the window of a men's shoe store. He groaned loud enough that a couple passing on the sidewalk stopped in case he needed help.

"He's being a ninny," I said. "Everything's fine."

"Eleanor Bouvier, attending a ball. You know, I wasn't quite sure Susan Lee living with you was the right idea, but I take it back. I'm glad she's making you take a chance and getting you to meet people."

There were moments when his face became a wash of emotions. There was a bit of pain as he remembered rescuing me and then to our less than amicable first years. But ultimately, he cleared his throat and smiled, a genuine melt-your-heart kind of smile. The big lug made me blush without saying a word.

"Stop it! She basically threatened to get murdered if I didn't go."

Frank paused. He couldn't tell if I was joking or being serious. The man knew me too well to assume I joked.

"The murders," I said as if that explained everything.

I walked down the sidewalk while he followed behind. I finally heard him utter, "Oh." Nobody in New York City could have missed the press coverage at this point. We were facing a war overseas, and it was becoming clear there was a battle on our own soil, one waged in the shadows.

"Well, I think it's a marvelous idea. God knows you could use some friends."

Topic change. "When she mentioned that, I wondered, Frank, what if I could help?"

"You can't kill Susan Lee," he joked.

"You're insufferable. No, the murders. What if the ghosts showed me the next victim? Like, what if I went to the crime scene?"

"Has something changed? I thought they only showed you the future. Is there anything there that could help you see the future?"

"If the visions predict the future, could they reveal the past?"

"You're crazy for thinking about it. But, I didn't think I'd be having this conversation in the first place. Who knew I'd be watching over a girl who can see ghosts? Ghosts that show the future."

"Who watches over who?" By this point the roles had reversed. Frank did less of the watching and more often than not, I was the one making sure he stayed clothed and fed. I glanced over my shoulder and put my smile on display for him. Yeah, he was proud of that. I guess he should be. Without him I'd probably be dead— scratch that, I'd definitely dead by now.

"Look, I'm not saying you should go hunting down crime scenes trying to find a serial killer. But I know you'll do whatever the hell you want. Promise me—"

"I'll keep you informed of the situation. I haven't decided if I want to be a crime fighter yet."

"Yes, you have, you just haven't admitted it yet."

We paused in front of one of the high-end dress shops. This section of Manhattan was outside our normal stomping grounds, but if I attended Susan Lee's ball, I knew it'd be my only opportunity to play the part of a civilized lady. In the window, mannequins were dressed in lavish dresses that no average woman would be caught dead wearing.

Frank's brutish hands pointed at the tag through the glass. He stuttered as he tried to comment on the price. "Does that say forty-nine dollars? Eleanor, dear God, what have you been doing with your free time?"

"Do you really want the answer?"

"No. No, I do not. You know, you're enough to drive a man to drink."

"Frank!"

His sobriety had been a struggle with as many slips as successes. I'd spent my teen years rescuing him from Harry's and making sure the tab was paid. Frank had watched his best friend, my father, die only to survive himself. Frank swore to him that he'd protect Benjie and me when he returned—at least he rescued one of us. Between survivor's guilt and raising a less than normal daughter, life had been difficult. When they wouldn't let him reenlist, he drowned his sorrows with whiskey.

"How are the meetings going?" I opened the door and regretted agreeing to the invite. Waves of perfume flooded from the showroom and my eyes twitched, tears threatening to smudge my makeup. It was a rare occasion I spent time applying eyeliner, but buying a fancy dress warranted the time.

"Fifty-three days sober," he said proudly.

"Good. Make it fifty-four and I'll buy you a cake."

"You're a tease. Now I want cake."

I paused just inside the store when I saw the shopkeeper. Her hair, perfectly pinned, and her makeup showed a masterful hand. I felt self-conscious, but in the back of my mind I knew I could punch her in the chest if she got smarmy with me. She judged me as she glanced down the sharp slope of her nose.

"Can I help you?"

My slacks were tailored to make them better hang off my hips, but I could tell she only saw a woman wearing men's clothes with a large brutish man in tow. This would be as painful as I feared.

"I'm looking for a dress for an event tonight."

"Oh." A single word. I surprised her by asking for something other than a job or to use the bathroom. She couldn't imagine somebody like me coming in and seeking to purchase a garment from her shop.

"It's a ball being held by a doctor. You might be able to tell, dresses aren't something I usually wear."

"If you go one block east, they have a selection a little more—"

When I pulled out the wad of twenty-dollar bills from my pocket, the woman's demeanor changed. I assumed she dealt with the eccentric wealthy elite of New York City. While I wasn't rich, I might be classified as non-traditional. Frank stifled a laugh, knowing full well I didn't like to deal with classism.

"When is your ball?"

"Tonight, at eight, so I guess I'll need it by seven."

"Miss, this isn't one of those department stores. Our seamstress hand sews our dresses." I caught her between wanting to shoo me away and desiring my money. I loved the predictable greed of mankind. Had I been thinking, I would have left several bills in my pocket so I could have pulled out a second handful.

"I guess your seamstress is the one I need to be talking to then. Bring her out." The woman thought I made a joke. I crossed my arms and cocked my head to the side, returning the dismissing look. "Shoo now, I want to speak with the seamstress."

"This is highly unorthodox." I lifted my stopwatch and flipped it open, making a slow and deliberate act of it. She took her cue. "I'll be right back."

The woman left through a door in the rear of the store. Frank chuckled at the absurdity while I started looking at the patterns laid out on the counter. There were a dozen lovely white wedding dresses sprawled across the table. The drawings of the women in the gowns were exquisite. The thought of finding a man and settling to rear children was not in the cards. How could I tolerate a man perpetually stuck in the now? What if our kids were cursed like me?

"You'd make a stunning bride."

"Frank…"

"You're not deciding today, but maybe someday, when the situation is right." His hand rested on my shoulder. He was the only man I needed in my life.

"Emma Jean is our seamstress." The woman's tone spoke the "negro" for her. I stepped forward, putting my back to little-miss-uppity and focused on the young woman no older than myself.

"Emma Jean, can you really make dresses like that?" I pointed to the counter. Her eyes remained fixated on a spot on the floor. It made me furious that it was the expectation. She snuck a glance at the garment and followed it with a brief nod.

"They're stunning." She tensed when I took her hand.

"We only make—"the clerk started.

"Hush," I pinched my fingers shut in the same manner you would use to silence a child. "It seems Emma Jean is the one making the finest dresses this side of Manhattan."

Her eyes were a beautiful shade of dark brown, filled with joy and heartache. It took a moment before I realized Emma Jean had stopped blinking. The ghosts appeared, each of them leading to a conversation with Emma Jean that resulted in the clerk degrading her.

The room darkened despite the light shining through the massive panes of glass. I was following Emma Jean down a sidewalk in a part of the city I hadn't seen before. There were young men sitting on the stoop, one of them smiled and waved while the other puckered his lips to whistle. She walked faster than I could follow until I stood still in front of a storefront.

The colors of the bricks were more vibrant than the rest of the street and inside I could hear a woman humming. A sign hanging in the window saying something in a language I couldn't read. I do, however, make out the single staff with a snake spiraling around the height of it.

The feeling in the pit of my stomach turned sour and I feared I might hurl. I snapped out of my trance and noted Emma Jean's blinking. I let go of her hand abruptly, sending the woman an awful message.

"Thank you, miss."

"Foolish me, I forgot to get a dress for a ball tonight. Can you help me out?"

"But our other patrons—" interjected the clerk.

"I'll make it worth both of your times."

"Sorry, but I can't," Emma Jean started.

"I can pay—"

"It's not about money, miss. I can't sew something that beautiful so quickly."

She's fearful, not of my displeasure but of the woman preparing to yell at Emma Jean for not obeying orders. I gave her a smile and a slight nod.

"I will be back, for my next ball." It was a lie. There was no chance I would return, not here, nor any other dress shop. But hopefully I could smooth over the tongue lashing she was about to receive.

"Wait," Emma Jean's face lit up. "A woman returned her wedding dress because she's with child. It's a beautiful gown that will make you irresistible. I can take your measurements and fit you."

"That would be lovely."

Emma Jean's eyes twinkled, excited at the prospect. I stuffed my money into my pocket and prepared for getting every inch of my body measured.

"And Emma Jean, is it possible to dye it powder blue?"

I expected more blood.

Frank tried to warn me, or at least prepare me for the gore. Where another man would shun me from seeking atrocities, he knew better. I had seen, no, experienced the brutality of men. Frank respected that. Instead of failing to deter me, he equipped me with knowledge. Even when I asked if he wanted to accompany me, he politely refused, claiming he had witnessed more than his fair share of unnecessary bloodshed.

Victory over the arrogant store clerk and the joy on Emma Jean's face bolstered my ego. I could do this. I could use the ghosts for something other than self-inflicted torture. Perhaps they would show me the next victim and give me a hint to the identity of the killer. The task was herculean to say the least, even if I knew the exact man responsible. How would I convince an officer? I'd worry about the last part later, right now, I needed to focus on using the ghosts for something positive.

The alley was wide enough for trash cans to be stacked, but if I reached out, I could almost touch the bins on each side. If I were to be a killer, I would lay in wait in a space just like this. If I couldn't find a person straying from the street, it'd be easy to drag them into the shadows. The thought hung in the air for a moment.

I turned, facing the entrance. "If I were walking along, why would I come down this street?" Peering down the alleyway revealed a lack of doors. At the end it connected to another alley. "No smart person would venture through here."

The chalk markings were thickly lined around where the victim had been discarded. I wish I had seen the man, to figure out which way he had faced. I assumed, based on the angles of his limbs, he'd fallen on his back, which would have left him facing the street. He hadn't walked down the alley, they had pulled him in.

On either side of the chalk drawing, there were trashcans where a killer could hide, waiting for his victim to walk by. I imagined the man with slicked brown hair and a perfectly docile face. For a man to kill this many people and not leave evidence, he was smart and meticulous. The ghosts were smarter.

Gravel bit into my knees as I knelt next to the chalk outline. Touch often spawned the ghosts, causing them to burst forward and show me the future. I laid my palms on the outline. My body tensed as I attempted to physically thrust my ghost outward. It wasn't often that I wanted to see my own future, but it'd give me a concrete path to follow. It was bad enough to know the events of every person around me, turning it on myself made me feel claustrophobic.

My arms shook before I sighed.

"Dammit." I didn't know what I hoped to uncover, or if I'd find anything at all. I thought it was childish for me to come here. In the past, the ghosts showed me gruesome stories, and I tried to stop them from coming true. I learned they tortured me, showing me the future and making sure it remained inevitable.

The chalk was less of a powder, almost creamy, leaving chunks of white on my hands. I was dirty already, so I might as well take the plunge and cover myself in the nastier grime. My palms rested on the blood.

The ghosts appeared, a man dropped a bag of trash into the bin. Despite my position on the ground, my ghost followed. I watched through otherworldly eyes, following him as he walked to the street. There were thousands of ghosts. Each person had a trail of specters in front of them, showing me seconds and minutes into their futures.

I had seen ghosts like this before in the hospital. There, they seldom slept and more often than not, I found it difficult to discern ghosts from their owners. Whatever medication they forced down my throat kept me sedated, but left me unable to sleep. It was impossible to say no to the ghosts, and without me fighting, they showed me the future days, weeks, even years away.

I followed the mundane gentleman from the bin to the street. As he walked into his store, another ghost caught my attention. I continued following, some sense of urgency deciding this woman was important. She veered right down a smaller side street. Her ghost faded until another man appeared, the same effect urging me to follow.

In the years since the ghosts first manifested, I had seen horrific things. I watched people die, and despite knowing their death was coming, fate brushed me aside and refused to let me intervene. But unlike those moments, I now felt exhilarated, almost as if I was in control. Never had I walked this far from my body, nor had I experienced the tugging sensation drawing me to particular specters.

Down another side alley, the man faded from sight. No other ghosts remained, only mine left spinning, searching for answers. I knew without a doubt, because my future self stood there, shortly I would as well. Fate set me on a path and there was no point in resisting.

Between blinks, I snapped back into my physical self as if I hadn't gone traipsing through New York as a specter. Sitting upright, I pulled a handkerchief from my pocket and wiped the white and bits of red from my palms. When I finished, I tossed it in the bin and started on my route to where my ghost had gone.

There were few people on the streets, presumably most of them working at one of the factories making clothes for the soldiers or parts for the planes. I had considered participating, attempting to blend in with the other women, but more New Yorkers meant more ghosts. I didn't want to see into their futures to only know the woman next to me was in an abusive relationship, or that she cried at night over a dead husband. My emotional reservoir would never be deep enough for that level of assault.

I found myself in the alley. Nothing caught my attention. It was like any other dank narrow corridor in New York City. I wondered if this might be the location of the next attack. Could he be hiding behind those bins near the opposite exit? I wandered down the alley, the keys to my apartment protruding through my fingers should I need to punch my way to freedom.

"Dammit," I said, somewhat relieved and partially annoyed there was no dark-haired man hiding near the trash.

"I guess I tried," I slid the keys into my pants, ready to head home and prepare for the evening's events.

"No," I said in disbelief. Across the street from the alley, I recognized the storefront. A sign hung in the window, a single snake wrapped around a staff.

"There are no such things as coincidences," I mumbled.

Chapter Six

Three steps led to a landing, then five more, and I'd be attending my first ever ball. I had time to turn around, walk away, and come up with an excuse about how Frank needed me at the gym. I watched as phantoms of guests yet to arrive climbed the stairs and entered the ballroom. There were more than usual, a sure sign that I was getting too nervous to resist the ghosts.

The strings played an upbeat and jaunty number. It reminded me of the music my parents listened to while they danced in the dining room. Figures moved past the windows of the first floor, their shadows, backs straight and shoulders spread were almost intimidating. I refused to back down, swallowed by my insecurities.

The social elite in this area of Manhattan had more money than they knew what to do with. I didn't come here often, more like I avoided upturned nose and unwarranted snobbery. There was a lengthy list of things I detested, but arrogance without reason, that might be at the top.

A couple walked down the street, a lovely lady with her arm linked to a gentleman in a finely tailored suit. I would never admit it out loud, but I was self-conscious when I saw the lavishness of her dress. The women must use these opportunities to play out a scene from Hollywood. The fabric emphasized all the right curves. More than that, she carried herself as if she belonged. I could almost imagine seeing her getting out of bed and slipping out of her silk nightgown to put on the dress to cook her husband's breakfast. I, on the other hand, felt like a fish out of water.

Emma Jean had been amazing. Not only did she bring me the garment, but she was so excited by her efforts she promptly asked if she could stay to see when I put it on. Her energy was electric, and I was more than proud to show off her exquisite detailed work. She had taken the creation, a wedding gown, fitted it to my body. Most importantly she dyed it the perfect shade of powder blue. The moment I slipped it on, I knew people would say I was beautiful and pretty. In this perfectly tailored dress, I experienced a subtle power.

Her eyes lit up as I walked out of my bedroom, her lip fought to stay neutral but lost the battle. Her expression, the satisfaction and the outstanding work, *that* made me feel powerful. My fingers laced between hers and I smiled. Smiling is not my default, but there was something enchanting about her creation.

"Miss Bouvier," she started, "what are we gonna do about your hair and makeup?" Her assistance might be the only reason I didn't accidentally poke my eye out while applying eyeliner. If I didn't know better, I would think Emma Jean was more excited about this ball than myself. It took a moment for me to realize that I was going out to this over-the-top event thrown by obnoxious men and women who just wanted a reason to show the extent of their wealth. It saddened me knowing Emma Jean would never receive an invite.

"Can you help with my hair?"

She tried not to appear too eager.

I removed the dress and Emma Jean's eyes returned to the floor. "But first, Emma Jean, try it on. I won't take no for an answer." She raised an eyebrow, her face slightly puzzled. "I want to see how beautiful you are in your own creation." Emma Jean had looked ravishing. Of course she resisted, but I have a knack for being persuasive. If given the opportunity, I would have arrived at this event with her standing next to me. We would put on a show. Let them whisper, I thought, we would be the talk of the town for days.

The image of Emma Jean provided strength and reminded me I could be a queen. As the couple approached, I did my best to be a civilized lady. I gave a slight nod to the woman and a curtsy for the gentleman. They returned the gesture and continued up the stairs into the house. I knew I was busted when I heard giggling behind me and the quick clapping of gloved hands. I didn't need to turn around to see her.

"Susan Lee, if you ever speak of this—"

"As God as my witness, I never thought I would see the day." I wanted to get it over with. It would be painful, but there was no stopping. I turned. Susan Lee's smile spread from ear to ear, and she did everything in her power to not squeal out loud. She had won. I looked like a lady.

As the night carried on, the ghosts became overwhelming. The more I attempted to sort out what was real and what was a phantom, I started the downward cycle, spiraling until I was ready to hyperventilate. I tried to remain calm as I bumped into one patron after another moving my way to the entrance, but more people were blocked my exit. I turned right through a double doorway and at the end of the small hall, found a single door. Who cared where it led? I needed space, room to collect myself.

The handle turned and it creaked open. I slid inside, closing it quickly behind me. I rested my back against the door, eyes closed, steadying my breathing. It took a moment before I could focus on my surroundings. I had stumbled into the study. It might not be as decadent as the ballroom, but for me it was the jewel of the estate. Bookcases lined the walls, filled with tomes that I couldn't even imagine.

My ghost walked about the room, inspecting the books and moving toward a set of high-backed leather armchairs. I watched, curious to what my ghost might have discovered as it lifted a book from the coffee table. It shrugged, setting it down and finally knocked its knuckles on the giant globe between the two chairs. With a spin, the top opened, revealing a crystal decanter filled with bourbon.

I couldn't change fate, I could barely alter the future, but every once in a while I could sidestep it. I went straight to the globe, opened it and poured myself two fingers of alcohol. Once I spun it shut, the cover of a coffee-table book caught my eye. Three wavy lines, embossed in silver, protruded from its surface. I ran my finger over the three lines, curious as to what they represented.

"Dammit." The ghost had seen this, and my curiosity got the best of me, proving I couldn't deter fate. Lifting the book, I opened the cover, surprised to see our host authored this particular volume. Under Dr. Butler's name, Dr. Theodore Stewart, most likely another gentleman in the ballroom. I flipped to a random page where the tiny print spoke about obligations and duties. I set it down, more interested in the photographs resting on the fireplace mantle.

In one photo a man wore his doctor's jacket, proudly holding a diploma with another graduate from a university I had never heard of. The subsequent photographs told a story, him meeting a beautiful young woman and eventually their marriage. The gentleman from his graduation photo appeared at his wedding, a college pal turned groomsman.

The last few showed a picture of him with a baby in his arms. His expression in each of them was a bit alarming, almost as if neither he nor the mother quite enjoyed the experience. Where I expected a proud father to be joyously holding his newborn son, he remained stern as if he was preparing a list of groceries he needed for dinner.

The last few photos were different; a bit of mirth returned to his face, a smile and laughter with his wife. However, in none of the final trio of photographs were there any sign of their infant. I wondered if they might be amongst the guests?

The door gave a slight creak as a gentleman entered the study. I froze, a trespasser in this foreign kingdom, I prepared for exclamation about how I should not be in here. The worry only intensified as I turned to see him, the man from the photos.

"I'm so sorry."

He had a crooked smile on his face as he shrugged his shoulders. "No worries, lass. I saw you fleeing the ball, and I wanted to make sure you were okay. I have a knack for telling when a person has had enough of the stuffy individuals who frequent these soirees."

"Oh, it's not that. I get a bit skittish around large crowds."

"And yet here you are, in New York City. For somebody who doesn't like large gatherings, you certainly picked the wrong city to call home."

He wasn't mistaken. It would be easy enough for me to leave New York and retire to the farm. It might be filled with horrible reminders, but at least those ghosts were only memories haunting me. Here, it was an entirely new trauma. "There is a certain irony. I sometimes wonder if this farm girl should return to the wide-open spaces."

"A farm girl, that is quite intriguing."

"Says the man with how many degrees? I would think that a farm girl is the least interesting thing in this room."

"I'm Patrick Butler."

"Eleanor Bouvier."

"Any relation to Sinclair Bouvier? He's an outstanding surgeon."

"There is only me. No surgeons on this family tree."

His voice was dark, rich even, and when he laughed, I couldn't help but laugh with him. The moment I realized I let my guard down and acted like an average woman, I grew suspicious. Was he flirting with me?

"I must say this place, your home, it's more than I could ever dream. I expected you to be..." I had to search for the word, "stuffy."

"Touché. I have been accused of far worse. But alas, you're correct, this is a bit over the top, even for me. My parents, God rest their souls, were quite well to do and with their passing I inherited their money and their lifestyle."

"I only managed to inherit a penchant for crass humor and a mean right hook." I wanted to dislike the socialite. But he simply nodded to signal his listening, more than I could say for most men.

His specter stepped forward, arm bent in a manner suggesting he wanted to politely escort me back to the party. My ghost emerged and linked arms with his, and the two worked their way to the ball.

"What does your wife think of all of this?"

"Who do you think arranged this event? I'd have been quite happy working overnight at the hospital, but she insisted. There is one thing I've learned. Never deter a wife determined to make a spectacle."

"Smart and wise," I jested.

His laugh was disarming, draining my worry and replacing it with a gentle playfulness. He stepped to the side of the door, giving a slight bow as he bent his arm, just as the ghost had shown.

"What of your son? If he has nearly the charm of his father, I'd certainly like to meet him."

The doctor stiffened. He dropped his arm and stood upright, the muscles in his body tensing. I wasn't sure if I insulted the man with mention of his age. I had a knack for wedging my foot firmly in my mouth.

"He passed."

"Oh." My voice sank, obviously stepping into a less than delightful conversation. "I'm sorry."

"We should return."

The doctor held the door open, waiting for me to walk through. I lowered my eyes, fearful I had spoiled the gentleman's evening. As I walked by him, I realized something was off. Was this a situation that would ultimately result in a course correction to destiny, or were the ghosts wrong?

Even on second viewing, the sheer magnitude of grandeur left me breathless. The ballroom in the back of the house was two stories tall and sported four, no, five chandeliers. Tables were covered in white linens with matching plates and perfectly polished silverware, that showed more attention to detail than I could fathom. In a corner of the room, a string quartet filled the air with a touch of magic. I worried I had fallen asleep and now resided in a childhood fairytale.

The ghosts had quieted to a dull roar. I could make out several moving to the dance floor and a couple laughing while they held wine glasses. The level of sophistication was something I had only heard whispers of, and somehow, I, Eleanor Bouvier stood in the middle of the opulence.

Outside this room, down the hallway lined with dark woods and through a set of doors filled with ornate glass, a killer stalked the streets. More than that, across the ocean, men fought a war to protect the safety of American citizens. Here, it looked as if they had forgotten the struggle endured by many New Yorkers—the food rationing, or the number of bodies filling our cemeteries. The people at this event were left untouched by such realities. It was enough to wipe away the princess's story.

"Eleanor," Susan Lee tapped me on the shoulder, and as I turned, she gave a curtsey. I couldn't help but smile, her chipper disposition and insistence on spreading cheer managed to break down my walls.

"Eleanor," she said with a hiss and curtsied again. It took a moment before I realized I hadn't returned my end of this social obligation. I held the edges of my dress and lifted it slightly as I gave a low and deep curtsey. Susan Lee clapped her hands. I truly believed she accepted full credit for this transformation. I wouldn't deny her the triumph.

"Did you walk in with Doctor Butler?" She leaned in close, whispering in my ear. "He has a wife."

Susan Lee's subtle attempt at reminding me the man was off-limits was a slight jab at my loose morals. From her perspective, my occasional *guest* was borderline blasphemous. While I enjoyed a romp now and then, Susan Lee was busy praying that the men would return from the war so she might find herself a husband.

"It wasn't like that. He was being a gentleman and making sure I was okay. Speaking of, do you know what happened to his son? I might have unwittingly offended the man."

"Are you sure it was an accident?" Susan Lee knew me well enough to know my mouth spoke before my brain could rein it in. "I've never heard him speak of a child. He mentions his wife frequently, probably to keep the nurses from fawning over him. But not a son."

A gentleman standing near the tables stared at the two of us. I was about to cock my head to the side when his ghost boldly walked in our direction. He would most likely offer a horribly crass line about us being beautiful women. The transparent version bent at the waist in a graceful bow. I waited for Susan Lee's ghost to emerge, but like always, her specter eluded me.

"Susan Lee, there is a handsome bachelor who has had his eye on you since we've been talking." She started to turn and I grabbed her shoulder. "No, he's going to come here and court you. A lady deserves nothing less."

"Eleanor," she said with a gasp. "When did you start paying attention to the social nuances of courtship?"

I ignored her disbelief. She was right, sort of. I paid attention, I just didn't want to participate.

"Hello, miss." His voice was almost as dashing as his manners were proper. "I was wondering if you would do me the honor of joining me on the dance floor?"

The ghosts didn't lie. As she looked over her shoulder, giving me a shocked smile, I had to chuckle at her delight. I should never have been friends with a God-fearing woman fixated on the opinions of others, but she filled my heart. She spun about with the young man, and I knew Susan Lee would always be like a sister to me.

"I apologize for my icy demeanor earlier."

Doctor Butler had snuck through the crowd to stand at my back. I didn't turn, instead enjoying the graceful strides of Susan Lee and her suitor.

"I lost my brother and the grief nearly consumed my mother. You do not need to apologize." Other than Frank, nobody knew the history of my family. In a single phrase, I confessed more of my truth than I had anticipated.

"I am sorry for your loss. It must have been—"

"Please, let us not spoil an otherwise magical evening with discussions of sorrow."

He paused long enough that I looked over my shoulder to see if he had slipped back into the crowd. He smiled and gestured to the dance floor.

"Would you do me the honors?"

"What would your wife say?"

"You'd be doing her a service. She prefers to socialize with the other wives."

"I'm not sure I could follow." I could throw a devastating punch, even toss a man against a wall, but graceful, that wasn't exactly my specialty. If he needed a sharp tongue and a string of insults, I was his girl, but a trophy to parade on the dance floor, that was not me.

"And for a moment, I thought you were going to demand that you lead."

He walked to the edge of the floor and gave a slight bow, making the invite a formal affair. His right eyebrow rose as he held the position, waiting for me to make a move. I surrendered and followed him to the floor. With the amount of money spent on the dress and the effort Emma Jean had put into my hair, the least I could do was pretend to enjoy myself.

Butler's ghost stood face to face with mine and after some awkward missteps, it almost appeared as if I might sort out how to dance. I watched for a moment, observing the feet where I could until I caught onto the pattern of steps.

The real Doctor Butler stood upright, hands in position for me to join. My right hand in his, with my left resting gently on his shoulder as he guided his free hand onto the small of my back. The force of his pull almost made me trip. He expertly led, pulling me along for the ride. By the first rotation my feet fell in line and I moved with the man as if I had been dancing for years.

"They're all watching," he said in a low whisper. "They will talk about the woman in the powder-blue dress for days."

He spun me under his arm, giving me the chance to see the women gather and watch the spectacle from the edge of the dance floor. Their eyes were a mix of jealously and admiration as he pulled me back into position. Susan Lee would cackle loudly if she could feel the pride in my bones. For the first time in my life, I was envied, and I liked it.

For tonight, I was okay with being a princess.

Chapter Seven

The champaign left me tipsy. Between the dancing and flowing spirits, I felt almost giddy. The string quartet had slowed their tempo, and the dancers grew more intimate. Almost two hours later, and the gentleman who'd first asked for Susan Lee's hand in a dance continued wooing her. I might not see her ghost, but with some effort, I could find out if he was more than a dandy looking for a roll around in the sheets.

The ghosts came and went, silenced by the alcohol's dizzying effects. I couldn't remember the last time they left me alone. In truth, it had been some time since I enjoyed myself. The people crowding the dance floor weren't nearly as intimidating as they were when the evening started. I understood the constant need for alcohol Frank experienced.

Ha, unsuspecting fools.

I spun about in my chair, the room spinning more than I expected. I had thought somebody spoke to me. When the ghosts demanded my full attention, they could make noise, but even then, it was hard to hear individual words. Typically, when I could hear them, something awful was about to happen.

Who keeps this much money in their wallet?

I sat upright, certain I heard the voice of a young man. I took a deep breath and clenched the muscles in my arms, trying to summon the ghosts. A single ghost moved from the dance floor into the area near the chairs. The phantom belonged to a man, only a year or two older than myself. He paused, scanning through dollar notes before sliding it in his trouser pockets.

"Curious," I said. He pulled back the sleeve of his jacket for a moment, revealing several watches. "A thief! Tonight just got more interesting."

The owner of the ghost stepped off the dance floor, following the ghost's predictions. When he lowered his sleeve again he stopped. Unlike the general roundness of the men at the ball, this man was slender, his chest just shy of being called broad. His eyes met mine, and he realized I had discovered him.

Shhh, you saw nothing.

I heard the man's voice as clear as if he was whispering to me. His lips didn't move. At first, I thought he might be standing next to me and I was seeing an opaque ghost across the room, but it was indeed the young man. All the other ghosts vanished as my own emerged, barreling through the tables to meet the boy.

"You're…" He appeared dumbfounded and as I watched through my ghost's eyes, I couldn't tell if it was from fear or amazement. His hand reached out, passing through my ghost. I gasped, realizing he could see my future self. Never had another person seen the transparent specters that haunted my every waking moment.

You can see me?

"You can hear me?" His voice held a bit of wonderment. Hear? I didn't quite understand. Something about his gift must have differed from mine. I had a lifetime of questions, and for the first time, there might be another soul who could answer them.

I need to speak with you. His hand moved to my ghost's cheek, and I swore his fingertips grazed my skin.

"My wallet," an older gentleman cried. My ghost vanished. I remained in my seat. The man's statement caused a chain reaction of men reaching into their jackets, searching for their own wallets. A grumbling washed through the crowd.

I need to go. Stay beautiful, Kitten.

He maintained a slow pace, but still moved with a purpose as he headed toward the front doors. I had questions. I had no idea if he had the answers, but if somebody else could see the ghosts and not panic, they knew more than me.

Following, I stepped around tables and women inspecting their clutches to determine if anything had been stolen. I made it to the lobby before I decided I'd never be able to make pursuit in my shoes. Kicking them off against the wall, I started in a run, ducking under a man retrieving his jacket from a server. The door hadn't shut yet as I barreled through, looking for the direction the young man took.

"Did you see that thief?" An older gentleman with only half a head of white hair scoured for the pickpocket. I shrugged, unsure myself. My ghost continued running, turning right, robbing me of any choice.

"Is that him?" I lied, pointing left.

He started down the stairs and as he stepped onto the sidewalk he wove between cars as he went along. I ran. I followed the direction my ghost demanded and only a few yards ahead of me, it ran at the length of the block, chasing the shadow of a smallish man.

"Stop," I yelled. He turned right, and I followed suit. Once I reached the alley, I found there were too many directions he could have proceeded. More than a dozen entrances entered into the gardens of row houses.

My ghost jumped out of my body, showing me where I'd eventually run. I gasped as another ghost appeared, followed by a third. Never had there been more than one version of myself at a time. I tried to sort through which one I'd inevitably follow. All three faded until I was left alone, panting at an uncertain future.

"I," deep breath, "saw more than one future?"

My night went from being a debutant rubbing elbows with the rich elite of New York City and now I stood barefoot in an alley. Five minutes ago, I had been a singular oddity in the world, forced to endure demons in solitary. Now, I had proof there were more like me. Something about this teased the ghosts until they revealed something I'd never seen before: choices.

Chapter Eight

Days passed since discovering I lived in a haunted house. The ghosts hadn't returned, but I knew they were there, hiding. Momma left the hallway light on with our door open wide. I wouldn't tell him why, but in case they came again, I slept tightly gripping Benjie's arm.

I spent as much time outdoors as possible, climbing the tree in the backyard, where I wedged myself into a spot where the trunk split into three. Momma hated when I climbed the tree, worried Benjie would try. But she let me stay there while I practiced my spelling words.

"Ellie, come play with me," Benjie whined.

The adjacent farms were older families, their kids were grown up and working in the fields. When Poppa left, they struck a deal to tend our crops while the adults were gone. I never understood why he had to leave, but the neighbors got to stay. Benjie was too young to save America, but our neighbors were close to Poppa's age.

"Pleeeeeeease," he begged.

"You're worse than the cat, Benjie."

"Ellie, I'm bored. Come play with me."

I etched the letters onto my small chalkboard. B-O-R-E-D. If I didn't climb down, he'd go crying to Momma, and then she'd stand on the porch with a disapproving face. She never yelled, not at Benjie and me, but the scowl she mustered was almost as terrifying.

"Fine, I'm coming." I tossed my supplies onto the grass and scooched to the edge of the tree. I jumped, careful to make sure my dress stayed in place. Benjie jumped up and down clapping his hands, excited that he had somebody to entertain him.

"What should we play?" I asked.

"Cowboys and Indians!"

I shook my head. "You are not tying me up!" I eyed my copy of *The Wonderful Wizard of Oz* and tried to think of a make-believe game we would both enjoy. I liked the story, a young girl whisked away to a magical land where she makes new friends. Poppa had read it to me a hundred times. Now, when I turned the pages, I heard his voice.

I bent low and picked up one of the many sticks surrounding the tree. "Do you want to be a knight? You have to promise to protect innocent people from dragons."

Benjie's eyes lit up. He nodded, his little body shaking with excitement. "Get down on one knee, so I can make you a knight."

"Who are you?" He asked.

"I'm the queen, of course. I'm going to make you a knight so you can defend my kingdom from dragons."

He knelt on the grass. I gently touched the stick to one shoulder and then the other like my teacher had shown us in class. She said once that when men were knighted, they swore to protect their king and queen. I turned over my sword, handing it to Benjie as he stood.

"What do I do now?"

"You protect me, of course, silly." The giggling started the moment he spun around, swinging the stick wildly back and forth. I would never let him have a real sharp object, but he deserved credit for his enthusiasm.

"Look here, Benjie. Do you see that?" I pointed to the ground where the roots of the tree snaked in and out of the grass. "That's a dragon footprint. I bet he's hiding around here somewhere."

He roared, jumping in my way, one hand pushing me back while the other prepared his sword for a thrust. We walked quietly around the trunk, careful not to wake the beast. I let out a yelp, ducking behind the tree.

"What, Ellie?"

"Over there," I pointed to the sheets hanging on Momma's clothesline. "It's the dragon's cave. I bet he's in there protecting his treasure."

Benjie stood tall, his head reaching my shoulders. A quick salute, he held up the stick, jumping to spin about. The little booger made me laugh as he tried to walk softly, taking comically gigantic steps. He approached the first sheet blowing in the wind. He squatted close to the ground, hopping into the air like a frog.

"I'll protect you, Ellie!" The stick smacked against the cloth as he fought against an invisible serpent. He argued loudly with his make-believe foe. The sword fight turned into him shouting at the dragon to go away. I'd had enough, I was not a princess to be rescued, I was a queen.

Picking up a small branch from the ground, I lifted it over my head as I charged into the cave, yelling. I stood in front of Benjie, my sword raised. "You can't have my brother!"

"Ellie, that's not how you play. I have to save you."

"Sorry, Benjie, nobody saves Queen Ellie but herself!"

He whined and stomped his feet, his bottom lip pushed out in a pout that always won Momma's affection. I made a chopping motion with my weapon and fell to my knees. I growled. "Benjie, I can't stop the dragon by myself. I need you to help me."

"I'll save you."

"We'll save each other." He hardly noticed the difference as he started swinging his sword. We danced around in between the sheets for the next few minutes, chasing a dragon too scared to fight.

"I got him! Benjie, hit him in the chest and our kingdom will be safe." And with a final stab of his mighty sword, we defeated the dragon. Benjie jumped up and down, singing a song about how he killed a dragon.

The laundry flapped in the wind, and for a moment, I could see the porch. At the top of the steps leading to the kitchen stood the white ghost of my father. His hands rested on his hips and a big smile slowly spread across his face. There were pictures of Benjie and me in the house, but only a single photo of Momma and Poppa tucked away in her nightstand.

"Benjie, do you see Poppa?"

"Poppa? He's protecting America. You know that, silly."

"I mean," I pointed to the steps, "right there. Do you see something that looks like Poppa?"

He held a hand over his eyes, leaning forward like the porch were a thousand miles away. Benjie raised an eyebrow, while circling his finger around his temple to let me know I was crazy. He stopped when I gave him a slight shove.

"I'm going to tell Momma."

"Tattletale."

The man blew away, leaving nothing behind. I didn't want to go in the house. I didn't want to see anymore ghosts. Momma refused to believe me when I told her what I saw. A bad dream, she said. It wasn't though, our house was haunted, but nobody believed me.

"Poppa?" Benjie's voice was the calmest it had been all day.

A sheet tried to wrap itself around me as the wind picked up. I batted at it. Frustrated, I pulled it off the line, peeling it off me and throwing it to the ground. Benjie ran toward the house, his arms stretched outward.

Looking toward the house, I gasped. Poppa. Standing right where the ghost had been seconds earlier. He rested his hands on his hips and smiled at the little booger running toward him.

"Poppa," tears filled my eyes, "is that you?" It wasn't real until Benjie jumped into his arms. A ghost wasn't holding the little booger, it was our dad, back from protecting America.

I couldn't be scared of the house, not with him there. If something bad hid inside, he'd protect us. I dropped the stick and ran toward my father. Momma stood in the doorway. Her hands covered her mouth but failed at hiding her tears. I jumped the steps two at a time. He dipped, scooping me up alongside Benjie, squeezing us both tightly.

"You're real," I cried.

"Of course I am," he kissed the top of my head and did the same thing to Benjie.

"Ellie." Benjie leaned back from Poppa's chest. He cocked his head back, thinking really hard about something. "How did you know Poppa was home?"

Chapter Nine

A light rain had left the ground littered with puddles. I didn't dare return to Doctor Butler's party, my stockings in shambles and the edges of my dress drenched. My entire body was on fire, charged from a chance encounter with a pickpocket. I couldn't go home, not until I talked to somebody.

Frank lived in a small one-bedroom apartment not too far from my own. He first came to New York City to pursue his career as a firefighter. It was hard to recall how cramped the space had been. He'd given me the bedroom while he slept on a cot in the living room. It was almost as tight as our purse strings, but we made due.

I walked up to the stoop. A single light remained on in the hallway, making it almost bright compared to the darkened streets. The man on the first floor must be up smoking one fag after another, the scent leaking from under the door enough to make me cough. It served as a reminder. I'd have to speak with Susan Lee about her habits less she become this man.

I tiptoed through the hallway past the mailboxes and up the stairs. Frank's door was first on the left, a massive green rectangle. I went for my pocket where I kept my keys and remembered I had forgotten them at the party. On my tiptoes, I ran my fingers along the doorframe until the key slid off, clanking on the floor.

I grabbed it and opened the door, sliding it in as quietly as possible. There might be a bedroom with a more than comfortable bed. But, I had no doubt that Frank would be curled—

A slow, deliberate click had me freezing in my steps. The room was a sea of black. A thousand possibilities rushed through my head and before I knew it, I could see ghosts despite the lack of light, mine and Frank's.

"Frank," I said.

"'Nore? What the hell are you doing sneaking in at this hour?"

"Do you have a damned gun? When did you get that?"

"This thing?" I'm sure he pointed to it even though we couldn't see. "One of the guys at the gym. I don't know if you've heard, but there's a killer out there. I wanted to make sure you were protected."

The lights kicked on and Frank sat on the edge of the couch with his arm partially extended and the gun aimed toward the ceiling. He eased the hammer back on the weapon. I was flattered, but did he really think I'd be able to handle a .357 in a pinch?

"He couldn't find anything bigger?"

"Are you barefoot? What happened?" Frank set the gun down on the hand-me-down coffee table in the middle of the living room. He approached me, inspecting me, assessing the damage.

"I'm fine. I lost my shoes when I started chasing him."

"Him? What are you talking about?"

"We need coffee." Those three words served as the universal statement that it would be a lengthy conversation. Frank returned to the living room to put on clothes while I stepped into the compact kitchen. Well-rehearsed, I flipped on the stove while grabbing the kettle.

"You were at the party with Susan Lee?"

"Yes. I—"

"Is it weird for me to say you look stunning?" Leave it to Frank to make parenting awkward. The man had no problem with teaching me how to throw a punch or break a man's arm, but the moment it came to womanly topics, he stuttered. We neared the day I'd have to talk to him about finding a lovely lady for companionship.

"Thank you."

"Start at the beginning, what did you find at the crime scene? Did the ghosts show you anything?"

"I'm certain whoever killed the woman pulled her from the street. I was surprised by the lack of blood. There should be more gore, right?"

"Be thankful," he replied. Frank had seen more than his share of dead bodies.

"I tried to make the ghosts appear by touching the chalk. I had no luck until I touched the blood. It wasn't exactly the highlight of my day. The ghost appeared, and I was able to follow it for quite a distance this time."

"Did you find anything useful?"

"The ghosts didn't show me anything, but it led me down an alley to a store. I think it's a medicine shop of some sort. I saw the same storefront when I had a vision of Emma Jean."

"Hmm." Visions and ghosts, and he didn't try to explain away my craziness. I could only imagine if I said these words to Susan Lee. Her church group would hoist me onto a pyre, praying as they set me ablaze for being a witch.

"Are you going to follow-up?" he asked.

"What harm could there be in visiting a local doctor for a touch of the vapors?"

"Be careful, Eleanor," he warned. "I know telling you to stop is futile, but don't do anything that puts you in harm's way."

"Yes, Frank."

"If something comes up, get me and I'll go with you."

"Yes, Frank."

"You're going to ignore my warnings, aren't you?"

"Yes, Frank."

I didn't need to see him to know he was wiping his eyes as he shook his head in disbelief. "Good Lord, you'll put me in an early grave." Did other parents hover over their kids like this?

I filled the kettle and placed it on the burner. He had exactly two of everything, two cups, two plates, two bowls. I wondered if he kept them for when I visited or if the military had created a monster only comfortable with a set routine. I suspected the latter, but I found his resistance to change endearing.

"How was the party?"

I tapped my fingers on the counter, counting down the seconds until the kettle whistled.

"Truthfully? It was a delight." Steam pumped out of the spout. "I danced, Frank. Me, dancing, who would have thought it?"

"What have you done with 'Nore?"

"Hush your mouth. The man holding the party, Doctor Butler, escorted me onto the dance floor and it was almost like a fairytale. I know, I'm still in shock myself."

"What about your *him*?"

I added two scoops of instant coffee to each mug and poured in the water before the whistling started. One black, one with cream. I opened the fridge and saw a single loaf of bread and a few vegetables nearing their expiration date. In the door stood one bottle of cream. Frank drank nothing but strong coffee. As I added cream to my cup, I smiled. Frank might not be my actual dad, but he was just as much a father by deed.

I walked out of the kitchen balancing the two cups, making sure not to spill the essential liquid. Handing him his cup, I sat on the couch opposite him. I tucked my legs under me, sipping until the tips of my lips burned.

"Are you ready for this?"

His eyes were staring at me as he took a gulp from his cup. He ignored the piping hot coffee and drank as if it were water from the tap. Frank had a knack for being quiet when necessary. He must have been single by choice because he was truly the ideal husband. No man could court me and overcome the impossibly high bar Frank set.

"The ghosts showed me a man, maybe a year or two younger than me. I could see him inspecting money and an arm with more than one watch."

"A pickpocket? I'm not surprised, where better to make fast cash?"

"There's something else." I had to think of how to explain it. Even as I formulated the words, it sounded make-believe. "When he spoke, his lips didn't move, but I could hear him."

Frank's eyebrow lifted, perplexed by my statement.

"You know how you just thought, 'What is she thinking about' but I couldn't hear it? Imagine if I could. That's what happened."

"So you can read people's thoughts too? That could be—"

"No," I corrected. "Not me. He can make other people hear his. He spoke to me without using his mouth."

"Oh." Frank did his best to process the news. He had the same expression as when I discussed the latest music on the radio. There was a grasp of the information in a broad sense, but he'd never completely realized the importance. I appreciated the effort none the less.

"He saw my ghost."

That statement caused him to spit coffee back into the cup. Frank knew about the ghosts before he rescued me. My father confided in the man with what he called my "extraordinary gifts." Again, he probably thought it was a dad making grand statements about their kid. After a few months of living with me, he started to believe. Since then, speaking of things he couldn't see was as natural as sharing small talk about the weather.

"Are you certain?"

"He reached out to touch my ghost. He spoke to it as if it were me. Frank, this man wasn't the least bit scared by it."

"This, pickpocket."

"Stop judging. I've done far worse than liberating expensive trinkets from rich people."

"Yes, which I'm none too thrilled about either."

I was too excited to let the jab at my ethics derail me. "What if he knows more about the ghosts? What if he can control them? I'm not sure, what if he—"

"That's a lot of what if's? Stop letting your mind race, you don't know exactly what happened. Let's start with what is concrete." Frank's military and firefighting training started. Assess the situation, state the facts, act on certainty. "He can see your ghosts. It means you're not the only person with gifts."

He continued speaking, but I ignored his words as I focused on that one statement. I wasn't alone. If there was another person out there, there might be more. I couldn't help but imagine an entire community of people able to see the ghosts. Perhaps they broke away from the future the ghosts revealed.

"One more thing, Frank," I had nearly forgotten in my zeal for cursed brethren. "I saw more than one ghost."

"I thought you saw hundreds of people's ghosts."

"No," I reached out, resting my hand clutching the handle of his cup. "I saw more of myself. I didn't see a single absolute future. There were three possibilities."

Frank set his mug on the coffee table and leaned back on the couch. We had discussed the implications of my visions. More than once, he listened to my frustration of not being able to change the expectations of fate. I didn't need to hear his thoughts to know he replayed countless nights where I cried over a tragedy I couldn't prevent.

His words were just above a whisper. "You're saying, the future..."

"Isn't fixed. I think." I finished.

Chapter Ten

The door to my bedroom swung open. I groaned, pulling the blanket tightly over my head, not willing to admit that it might be time to wake up, but Susan Lee refused to relent. Feet stomped toward the bed, and she wrestled with me for the covers, tearing them away, leaving me exposed.

"We need to talk, Eleanor Bouvier." When she used my full name, it served as a declaration of war. Short of tackling her to the floor, there was no way I'd emerge victorious in this battle.

"It's too early," I groaned.

"It's nearly nine in the morning. You wouldn't be hiding under the covers this late if you had come home at a reasonable hour."

I couldn't tell if it was concern or anger. Sometimes when Susan Lee got worked up, it slid between the two emotions. With hands on her hips and a fresh face of makeup, she stood ready for battle.

"I was with Frank. He was tempted last night, and I offered to sit with him." They weren't quite lies, more like slight alterations of the truth. They came naturally, to the point where I had to remind myself I wasn't speaking the truth.

"Oh."

Whatever caused her flurry of emotions this morning washed away. I couldn't fathom what had the woman worked up.

"Susan Lee, what are you getting at?"

"I saw you chase that young man out of the ball. I picked up your shoes. You're welcome."

Did she storm into my room because she thought there was a boy in my bed? "I heard somebody say their watch had been stolen. He might have known something about it. I didn't want to let a thief get away."

"That's just foolish, Eleanor. He could have been a ruffian."

"He wasn't."

She started pacing. Could she be so worried about me chasing a burglar into the street? Her reaction was more intense than the situation warranted.

"Did you catch him? Did he do it?"

"I did, and no, he didn't." I'd have to remember telling her this lie. Coming up with creative explanations this early in the morning required a mental note for later.

"You nearly scared me to death, Eleanor. I came home, and you weren't here, and I..." her voice cracked. "I called the hospital yesterday to make sure you hadn't been hurt."

Susan Lee could overreact to small things, but this was more than I expected. She sat down on the edge of my bed, pulling her housecoat tightly around her body.

This wasn't going away, so I sat upright, scooting up against my headboard. I had only gotten home a few hours ago, just as the sky changed color before sunrise. I had been exhausted, not from the dancing or chasing the pickpocket, but from the electric sensation I had thinking about the possibilities opening before me.

"They found another woman dead." I suddenly realized the overreaction to my disappearing in the middle of the evening. "They said she was a young woman only a few blocks from the party."

I grabbed Susan Lee's hand, gripping it tightly. "You don't need to worry about me, I can take care of myself."

"Perhaps you can..."

Oh. Apparently, I didn't know how to read my roommate's intent. The young God-fearing woman wasn't scared for me, she was terrified the body could have been her. I wish I could assure Susan Lee, promise her she'd die at the ripe old age of sixty, with her family showering her with love. I never thought the absence of ghosts would be a terrible thing, but right now, I wished I could see her future enough to speak with conviction.

"Anybody who knows anything knows I'd kick their asses if they touched you."

"Language!"

"I'd whoop them something fierce. Nobody touches the only person willing to put up with my shenanigans."

"It's not safe out there," she whispered, "for either of us. I wish this stupid war was over and the men were back. The streets would be safer with them here."

"When you leave the hospital, I want you to phone Frank at the gym. He'll send one of the soldiers to escort you home. I'll talk to him today, he'd be more than happy to make sure you're safe."

"What about you?" Sometimes, I wish the woman Susan Lee saw in me was real. I didn't know how to be docile or demure. If somebody grabbed me and attempted to drag me into an alley, I'd have no problem breaking their limbs.

"I'll be careful when I'm out."

"He left her right there in the open. He didn't even care if they found the body. What kind of sick person would do that?"

Her face transformed from the normal worry she carried in her brow to something darker. The killer had murdered four women and three men, and it appeared as if there was no attention to race, gender, or social status. I didn't say it out loud but seeing the soft brown eyes glaze over as tears formed, I knew I'd be the one to find the answer.

"Come here," I hugged Susan Lee, my only genuine friend. If she was terrified to live her life and the ghosts would not reveal her future, I'd have to find another way to help her. I had one lead. Hopefully, it was more than a dead end.

The bruise along the side of my face had gone from an angry red to bits of purple splotching. I found it foolish to spend so much time on my appearance, but I didn't want to be memorable, at least not today. What waited for me inside the pharmacy? I needed to get my intel and not draw more attention than necessary.

Reaching into my purse, I pulled out my compact, flipping it open and inspecting my handiwork. I powdered my face before applying a fresh coat of lipstick. Checking the tightly wound curls spilling down the side of my head and onto my shoulders, I looked like any other woman. If somebody were to describe me to the authorities, nothing would easily stand out, not even the dress I begrudgingly wore.

"You can do this," I whispered to myself. My sleuthing had gotten me to this point, but when I needed the ghosts the most, they deserted me. Part of this curse meant only knowing it sometimes. I hoped with the latest development I might have a modicum of control, but alas, the taunting continued.

The shop had the same staff of Hermes in the window. I eased the door open, the bell gently ringing above my head as I poked inside. Scanning the store for signs of an attacker, I made a note of the nooks and crannies I couldn't easily see. I stepped across the threshold.

It was smaller than I expected, not much larger than my apart-ment. Racks were spaced out along the far wall with a gigantic table in the middle of the room with various baskets covered with satchels. The entire shop had a fragrant smell of flowers and fresh herbs.

"I'll be away in a moment, child," came a raspy voice through a curtain on one side of the shop.

I inspected the closest rack, seeing the glass jars filled with different colored leaves inside. It took a second before I understood it was indeed a pharmacy, but not one that served pills and serums you might find at the hospital. My mother had been a nurse, but even with modern medical techniques, she swore a bit of rose water helped ease a headache or honey cured a sore throat.

"What ails you, child?"

A slender black woman poked through the curtain. She had a white shawl draped over her shoulders, contrasting against the dark-ness of her skin. I couldn't be sure, but I would guess she was closer to Frank's age than my own.

"Vapors. A friend suggested I come here."

"Hmm," she thought, "headaches, fatigue, dizziness?"

"Yes, ma'am."

"Don't you ma'am me, child. Please call me Claudette."

Her gown consisted of a dark pattern, without pockets. I checked both hands, making sure she didn't have any utensils that I might have to fear should I turn my back.

"Claudette, what is all of this?"

"Before men made pills, nature provided us all the healing we needed. We've forgotten what she is capable of. I like to think I'm helping people remember."

"My mother believed in natural medicine."

"Smart woman," Claudette said. "Let me see if I have something that can help these vapors."

"Do I detect an accent? French perhaps?"

"Oui," she said, "My parents emigrated from Haiti when I was a girl."

While she reached into jars, filling a small pouch, I walked around, smelling the herbs as I went. The table had a mortar and pestle, still filled with half-ground flowers. Claudette hummed as she moved, a melody almost as sweet as the room.

A thick book rested on the table, opened to a page with drawings of a plant I hadn't seen before. On closer inspection, I could see it contained recipes, except instead of food, it was for her particular brand of medicine. With the war draining resources from the states, I could understand why her shop thrived.

"No, something weaker," she mumbled as I tried to stay out of her way.

Claudette appeared to be nothing more than a woman trying to heal the sick. I didn't believe the ghosts led me here to only find a cure for the common cold. My fingers balled into a fist, trying to will ghosts to step outside the woman. I needed to know her future, how she connected to the murders. For all I knew, somewhere hidden under her gown, she had a knife and she'd kill me given the chance.

My ghost appeared, flipping through the pages of the book, and then continued a round of inspecting jars. I wanted to fast forward, see through my ghost's eyes, and find more information. The woman, however, provided more insight than my ghost.

"Put it away," she said, mildly annoyed. "Last thing I need is your angel bringing negative energy to my shop."

"What?" I didn't understand what she was talking about.

Claudette stared my ghost directly in the eye. She stepped in close, until there was only a whisker between them. She turned her head slowly cocked to one side as she tried to read me. With lips pursed, she shooed the space in front of her, hands passing through the specter.

"Don't play dumb, child. Put your angel away. I have no time for that nonsense. If you have a question you want answered, ask."

My poker face faltered at the woman's forwardness. My heart picked up speed, fueled by hope and a tinge of fear. The pickpocket had watched as my ghost attempted to predict his future. Twenty-six years of being alone. Two days. Two people. I tried to remain calm and not allow my eagerness to show.

"You can see the ghosts?"

"That is no ghost, at least not a spirit from beyond the grave. My people call it *ti-bon-ange*, the little angel. I have not seen one in a very long time." There was no pomp and circumstance about the otherworldly, just simple facts. Could this be why they led me here?

"I have so many questions." My emotions surged. I thought the pickpocket was the only other person who understood. But in less than twenty-four hours, I had found another person who saw the ghosts.

"Am I cursed?"

Claudette gave a slight smile. The white of her teeth shone against the rich darkness of her skin. "No, child. You're not cursed. You have a gift. Very few people can see ti-bon-ange. My mother could see them, her mother before her could as well. I could see them as a child, but alas, they are but a memory to me."

Was she being cryptic to be difficult, or was that just how she spoke? I had mixed feelings. On one hand, I wanted to hear more about these angels, but on the other, I didn't like somebody intentionally withholding information. I was going to shake the woman until she stopped.

"Then how could you—"

"I cannot see, but this does not mean I do not know. You have many questions, I understand. But what is the actual reason you have come to my shop? I take it, you do not suffer from the vapors?"

"No," I admitted. "The ghosts led me here. I think it has something to do with the serial killer."

"If you believe I am the killer, then you are mistaken. I would not harm the hair on a child's head."

"Then maybe you're the victim?"

"What do these ghosts tell you?"

My face turned red, too embarrassed to admit that I did not understand how to navigate this supernatural thing I could do. I gave a slight shrug.

"If I see something bad happen, I can't change it."

Claudette nodded as if she understood the nature of the ghosts. "A Cassandra, I see."

"That's not my name," I corrected.

"No, child. Cassandra had a similar gift. In Greek mythology, she had the ability to divine the future. She knew the fate of every person she encountered. However, when she spoke of it, they simply did not believe."

"Oh." I was embarrassed, not only because I didn't know about this woman from history, but because I hadn't thought to research these gifts. The New York Public Library was one of the largest in the world, and with all that knowledge, there must be some mention of these abilities.

"What happened to her?"

Claudette shook her head slowly. "Her lover's wife killed her. So I suggest you be careful who you bed. We wouldn't want the same fate for you."

She held out her hand, a white linen bag dangling from her finger. I took the herbs. "Sorry, but I'm not ill."

"I know, child." She clasped my hand, her palms extremely warm as she gave me a slight squeeze. "What ails you is as much a sickness as the chickenpox. This will help. Steep in a tea and allow the angels to speak through you."

I reached for my pocket, and she made a loud tsk-tsk sound. She took a step back and grabbed her recipe book, slamming it shut.

"Your soul may be weary, but this is only the beginning of your journey."

"I thought you couldn't see the ghosts."

"Ghosts? No, not anymore, child. But Claudette knows many things, Eleanor."

Chapter Eleven

Sweat permeated the air enough to make my nose scrunch up. Unlike Frank's gym, this building had the added benefit of a cool, damp feeling making me pull my jacket tighter. A hint of soy punctuated the nasty scent, serving as a reminder of the restaurant kitchen between the entrance and the stairs to the basement.

A network of hallways connected the basements underneath the buildings above. They strung lights along the ceiling, pushing the shadows into the corners near discolored boxes. A crowd cheered as I reached the bottom of the stairs. Even the massive metal door across from the stairwell couldn't contain the sounds of victory. Somebody had just become rich.

I assumed there were other entrances, part of a bootlegging enterprise during the days of prohibition. I knocked, my knuckles instantly regretting the force I used. A slit about eyesight opened and a set of disgruntle eyes stared at me, trying to decide if I should be allowed.

"Password."

"Rainbow tulips." There was a pause. "Jimmy, let me in or I'll whoop you again."

I couldn't hear him sigh, but I had a front-row seat for the rolling eyes. Metal ground on metal, the security bar being pulled away as he opened the door. The guard was intimidating until you caught him standing on a wooden box to see through the slit. Jimmy had a mean mug, but there wasn't enough of him to be fearful.

"Looking like a fancy dame today. Too fancy for this place." Jimmy gave me the once over, pausing at my chest. He whistled, and I considered clubbing him with my fist right then and there.

The corridor opened into a massive room. Despite the size, the low ceilings and the hundred or so men shouting at one another made it feel far too intimate. A man sat against the wall, his face bloody and his shoulders limp. I had watched the same man fight last week. In fact, he profited quite well. Now, with a cut eye and bleeding nose, he was a losing bet.

"Eleanor," said a man holding a wad of one-dollar bills in his hand. "You come to clean me out again?"

While he held nearly a hundred dollars in one of his hands, it was the several larger bills in his pockets that interested me. Paying Emma Jean her worth for the dress meant having almost no money for rent. I wasn't going to get a job, not with my skillset. Down here, however, in the fervor of adrenaline, the ghosts had a way of bene-fiting me.

"I hope so. Who's up next?"

"Big Mike versus Lito. Three-to-one odds in favor of Mike. You want in?"

I did. One of Frank's members had introduced me to the fight club when I beat him in the ring. He had suggested I take up fight-ing, but once I asked around, I couldn't find anybody to fight. Even amongst the underworld, hitting a girl seemed off-limits. Men beating other men, though, that was what we were all here to see.

The ghosts had entered the ring, and I watched them move swiftly, the distance between now and the future growing further and further from the present. Ultimately, the referee raised Mike's hand in the air. I only had to guess how much to wager on the man. If I bid too little, I'd be here all day. If I tampered with fate too much, I'd somehow lose my money. The trick was finding the happy number to ensure I walked away with a full wallet.

"Twenty on Mike."

"Going for the sure thing this time? You don't think Lito can make it?" He was goading me. He knew Mike would be the winner. I might take a risk later, but I needed a small win to get the ball rolling.

"Sure thing."

The bookie continued to take bets after I handed him money. Few of the men took more than a fast glance in my direction. While I wouldn't call this the most progressive gathering of New York's finest, I appreciated their ability to look past my gender and focus on my money. They'd only grumble when I left with a wallet full of twenties.

Moments later, two fighters entered the ring, a loose rope dangling between cement columns holding up the roof. The referee had a hand on each of their chests, running through the rules before he stepped back and bellowed, "Fight." It wasn't much in the way of drama. The entire match took less than three minutes. Mike's size and reach made him the favorite, and with a solid punch to the temple, Lito fell.

There were only three more fights, three chances to make my money for the rest of the month. Forty dollars in hand, I could easily double it, but picking the winner each time could draw unwanted attention. There were mobsters in the room, the ones in finely tailored suits capable of gunning me down in the street.

The second fight I lost ten bucks. The bookie gave me a slap on the back, offering to console me with a firm hug. I declined. The next bout, however, had four-to-one odds, and the ghosts revealed the winner in an upset was the scrappy underdog. I put down thirty dollars.

"It's your loss," he said, glad to take my money.

"You're all crazy for brawn. I like a man with fast feet," I gave him a smile and suggestive wiggle of the brow. He laughed as he scribbled down my bet on a sheet of paper. He continued walking through the crowd, shouting the odds, greedily pulling money from the hands of compulsive gamblers.

When the match started, I hoped it'd end quickly. The brutish man made heavy-handed swings, hoping to land a single blow. Moving swiftly, the smaller of the two dodged the slow swinging club-like hand. The faster fighter took every opportunity to dish out a quick thrust before stepping out of the way. The fight lasted nearly thirty minutes. Even the crowd hushed, saving their burst of encouragement for when the two traded blows.

The larger man slowed, losing momentum from overextending himself. The smaller guy didn't appear to be tiring. I commended his tactic, the same one I relied on when boxing. When I set foot into the ring, the men outweighed me by two or three times. A single punch could dislocate my jaw or break my arm. I knew when I was physically outmatched. Sometimes the best move was to be the last one standing, even if you didn't deliver the final blow.

A series of jabs to the big man's stomach had him buckling over, searching for something to grab onto. As the little man danced backward, his opponent fell to the ground, exhausted. I had just made enough money to consider it a successful outing.

The bookie handed me the roll of bills and I folded it into my brazier. I was about to inquire about the final fight, tempted to push my luck when I saw a face I recognized. The pickpocket moved his way through the crowd, bumping into patrons as he approached the ring. Unlike the ball, now he wore a simple t-shirt with suspenders holding up his khaki-colored trousers. I nearly stormed through the men, but held myself in check, worried that I would draw unnecessary attention.

I see you, I thought, yelling it in my head.

He was almost hidden from view, the taller men swallowing him. I couldn't let him escape, not without at least getting his name. If he hadn't seen me, at least I could observe him, possibly making sense of the kind of man I was dealing with.

As the next set of fighters assumed their positions, I drifted through the crowd, trying to find a vantage point where I could watch both him and the boxers in the ring. I got dangerously close to the men in suits. Several of them paid attention to me as I tried to ignore them. On the far wall from the door, I could see the pickpocket and a line of men standing shoulder-to-shoulder, already yelling into the ring.

The referee introduced the fighters and with a shout, the match started. Both of the men were evenly matched physically, and it was obvious they spent plenty of time honing their bodies. The pickpocket also honed his abilities, being jostled back and forth by the men cheering. I had no doubt that with every bump, his fingers skillfully found their way into pockets and wallets.

The ghost of an Italian man approached me, leaning in close to speak in my ear. If he wasn't part of the mob, I'd be shocked. I had garnered too much attention and now they wanted an audience. There were many things I could handle, the dead haunting me, hunting a serial killer, living with Susan Lee, these were a piece of cake. Getting away from a New York mobster, I had never heard of that happening.

There are two types of dangerous. One, the man trying to make himself bigger grand over-the-top actions. Two, those secure enough with themselves to remain a peaceful calm. The first is hazardous because they're more likely to do something stupid. The latter, because you're not quite sure what they're willing to do, but certain they will do it. He was definitely the latter.

"Mr. Bertolucci wants to have a word with you."

I nearly cursed out loud. I didn't want to speak to this guy, I certainly didn't want to talk to his boss. Sometimes, being a woman has its advantages. We can hide in our naïveté. "I'm all set, but tell him thank you." I knew it wouldn't work, the ghost made certain, but I couldn't help but try.

"That wasn't a question."

Everybody talks about blue eyes, like their pools of water, waxing poetic. They describe green eyes like emeralds. But brown eyes, they get a bad rap. His were a cross between a deep forest brown and glittering gold jewelry. Under different circumstances, I might've complimented them. Right now, I don't think a compliment would do much good.

He stepped to the side, letting me lead. He wanted to be at my back, partly so I couldn't run, also so he could ensure I didn't do anything to him or his boss. I considered it, but there were far more men here than I could handle. Frank taught me to learn my own limitations. Five mobsters surpassed my limits.

I glanced over my shoulder, looking past my escort to find the pickpocket prowling about another group of guys. The fight raged on, the two men furiously throwing career-ending punches. I feared my exchange with Mr. Bertolucci would give him the opportunity to get away before I could speak with him.

Mr. Bertolucci was a sizeable man. Even though his suit had been tailored for his body, he still managed to nearly bust out of the seams. He was either a chubby man returning to the gym or a muscular one that enjoyed food. Either way, it was obvious he commanded the respects of his fellow mobsters. It left me wondering, how one gets to be in charge of the mob. Is it a birth rite? A title bestowed upon a family? Or did he have to kill to obtain it? I did not want the answer to any of those questions.

We stood only a couple feet apart, but neither of us spoke. I assumed he summoned me to exchange words. But instead he studied my face as if he were trying to write it to memory. Had he glanced at my breasts or scanned me up and down, I would have thought him a pigheaded man. But as the crowd cheered for a well landed below, the tension between Mr. Bertolucci and I was thick enough to cut with a knife.

"Can I help you?" I broke our silence.

"What is a pretty dame doing in a place like this?"

"They won't let me fight, so I might as well gamble."

Mr. Bertolucci laughed despite the roaring men in the oversized basement. His laugh cut through the air. "Did you hear that, boys? She'd rather fight." His henchmen all gave a slight chuckle, but none shared in his laughter. Something bad was about to happen.

Look at who it is.

The voice of the pickpocket was a welcome distraction from my inevitable demise. He wasn't a friend, or even an ally, but he would have to do.

Help, I asked.

Me? What could I possibly do? The pickpocket had a twisted sense of humor.

Please, the word sounded desperate in my head.

"Quite the gambler, you are. Seems every time you show up, my coffers get lighter."

"I don't know how anyone loses money. The matches are unbalanced, your bookie talks too much, and a little of an intuition goes a long way." Either Mr. Bertolucci appreciated my bravado, or he was about to shoot me.

"You think you could—"

"There you are," the pickpocket sidestepped my escort, putting his arm around my waist, pulling me in tightly. There was no point in fighting it. I put my arm over his shoulders and gave him a tight squeeze.

"I told you, dear, read the match, inspect the fighters, and play the bookie." The pickpocket gave me a squeeze before letting it go to free up his hand to shake with Mr. Bertolucci. The mob boss didn't seem impressed, I think he disliked my beau even more than he loathed losing money. Perhaps this ally had been an awful idea.

Chapter Twelve

Mr. Bertolucci's eyes read as vacant. The mobster could have been thinking about the weather, the sociopolitical ramifications of a foreign war, or the best way to kill us without getting his suit dirty. The referee yelled, announcing the matches were closed, but this man, with his narrow gaze, cared about nothing other than me.

Can you hear me? I wasn't sure how this worked. It seemed the pickpocket could project thoughts when he wanted. Could he receive them as easily?

Your thoughts are garbled. You're new to this?

I didn't quite know what he was asking. New to being cursed, or new to having somebody speak into my brain?

Never mind. I can hear your thoughts when you address me directly.

What are we going to do? The situation called for more than my own abilities. My gifts weren't capable of handling this level of stress. The ghosts stood just outside of each mobster, doubling the expressionless men.

We'll be on our way.

"We'll be on our way." There was an echo when the pickpocket spoke. His words sounded from his lips, but they also reverberated in the back of my head. I did not understand what he attempted to do.

"You should be on your way." Mr. Bertolucci made a sweeping gesture with his hand, ending our audience.

"Boss." The man to his right didn't like the change of plans.

Mind your business.

"Mind your business." Each time the pickpocket spoke, the sound of his words seemed to penetrate my brain. He spoke commands. Twice now, men who wanted to harm me, listened. His gifts were amazing on their own, but I was beginning to see that while we might both be cursed, there wasn't much else in common.

They should let us go without a fight. But be quick. The more people I influence, the shorter the duration.

I didn't want to argue with him. I wanted to leave there as quickly as possible. He held his hand back, waiting for me to grab it so we could make our getaway. His abilities were frightful, robbing men of their freewill. I wasn't sure how far he would go. A pickpocket must already have a loose set of morals. But I grabbed his hand. There were answers to be had.

We didn't dawdle. He led the charge, moving at a pace that said we wanted to leave, but not so fast it would draw attention. I felt he frequently needed to make speedy getaways. I should scold him for his choice of activities and the company he kept, but the roll of bills in my bra reminded me we weren't so different.

Ghosts belonging to the gamblers and mobsters moved in and out of people as I scanned the room, ensuring none of them intended us harm. The thief didn't seem to notice, stepping through the specter of a man lamenting over the loss of his money. Could he only see mine? Why? The list of questions continued to grow.

We reached the metal door leading out. I couldn't hear the words, but the bouncer had already released the lock and opened our exit. He stood idle as we walked by, his face blank as the mobster. The pace quickened through the restaurant, and we burst through the rear into the alley. He only slowed when we stepped onto the street, finally releasing my hand.

"Are you all right?" he asked.

I didn't have any additional holes in my body if that's what he meant. He opened his jacket and inspected the half dozen interior pockets. I could see they were clumsily hand-stitched, a plethora of hiding places for his newly acquired loot.

"Who are you?"

Edward. His name echoed in my head.

"Stop that," I said. "It's like an echo inside my head."

He leaned against a street sign. He spoke and paused, shaking his head. He raised a finger in the air as if he was about to pontificate and then reconsidered. I was about ready to scream. The man's ability to liberate wallets might be his least annoying habit.

"You really are new to this?" His words weren't a judgment.

My ghost stepped out of my body, and I watched as his eyes fixated on the apparition. The phantom closed the distance and grabbed the collar of his jacket. He swatted at the specter, unsure of what was happening. I walked forward, overlapping my ghost, grabbing him.

"I have questions, and you will answer."

"Quite the brutish broad, aren't yah?"

"The only reason I was down there gambling is because they won't let women fight. You decide just how brutish that makes me."

He bit his lower lip, withholding whatever snide comment that settled on his tongue. He glanced back and forth, checking the street. "Fine, I like a woman who doesn't mind getting her hands dirty. We can talk, but not here."

"'Nore." Harry's voice held the same annoyance it always did. He wiped down the counter, raising his eyebrow just a nudge as Edward followed me into the bar. This pub was a family secret. To bring somebody here meant they were to be trusted.

"I don't think I've seen you dolled up in ages," Harry said with a bit of surprise.

"Special occasion."

Harry eyed Edward with a slight crook of the head. I gave a chuckle at the insinuation that this might be a romantic affair. "Underground boxing."

Harry popped the caps off two beers and set them down on the counter. He leaned in, close enough to whisper. "Frank will kill the man who showed you that place. He's a bit protective over you." Harry said the last part loud enough for Edward to hear.

He thinks of you as a niece. He wants to know who I am but doesn't want to deal with you lying.

Stop it, I shouted in my head.

Edward didn't understand the word. He explained how the patrons hoped my beau would put me in my place. He avoided saying it outright, but the two sitting at a table were staring at my chest. Edward had no boundaries with spying into the minds of those around him. I worried just how much he could read from me. Did the ghosts somehow limit how easily he could hear my thoughts?

I grabbed a stool furthest from prying eyes.

"How does a dame like you wind up in a place like this?" Edward made a gesture to the rest of the bar. "No offense," he said when Harry looked up.

"Remember, I know how to kill a man." Harry's smile punctuated the ease of which it could happen.

He's not lying. Edward's mental voice held a bit of shock.

I couldn't help but laugh. We might not be killed by mobsters trolling through the streets, but Edward, if he moved the wrong way would be thrown from the bar. It wasn't an accident that we wound up here. He had the upper hand, and I needed somebody I trusted at my back. Eventually I'd confide in Frank, but this interrogation was between Edward and I, for now, at least.

I waited for Harry to return to his end of the bar. Frank had urged me to tell the man about the ghosts, insisting that he was a person I could trust. If not him, then Susan Lee. The madness had spread through my family and I was the only one still standing. Frank respected my decision, even if he didn't agree with it. I don't know how he would take knowing two more people knew, both of them essentially strangers.

"Talk," I said as I took a sip of beer.

"About? How much do you already know?"

I gave a slight shrug. "I can see ghosts, they interact with one another. That's about everything I know." I omitted the part where they showed me the future. I might be willing to discuss our more unique traits, but I didn't trust Edward enough to put it all on the table.

Telepathy. He paused when I scrunched up my face. He humored me, speaking with his mouth. "That's what they call it. It's the ability to send and receive thoughts."

"Wait, what? You mean you can hear everybody's thoughts." I tipped the bottle back and started chugging. Beer might not be enough for this conversation.

"You can't?"

I garnered a smile from Edward as I set down the empty bottle. "Don't pull that macho male crap with me."

"Sorry. Yes, that's what it is. It's different for each of us."

"You know more people who can do this?"

He shook his head. I didn't need to read his mind to know something had happened. The curse, it affected more than just me. I stole his beer and took a sip before he could protest.

"I knew one. He's who showed me how to..." Edward pointed at the breast of his jacket. I was glad to know our social circles were both limiting. "He used to drink to quiet the voices. When he went to prison, he killed himself. I guess he couldn't handle being that close to people."

Stopping mid-swallow, I let the beer work its way down the back of my throat. I set it down on the counter. From the second I was old enough to open a whiskey, I did the same. Self-medicating helped keep the ghosts from showing themselves. I didn't particularly like being drunk, but I also hated being haunted during my every waking moment.

"Sorry." What else could I say?

"Don't be. He was a bit of an ass. But he taught me how to deal with this. I'm lucky I can turn it off."

"It's not the same for everybody?"

"Obviously not," he gestured to me. "He certainly didn't have the ability to do what you do. I'm not sure I could do that."

"What did you call it? Influencing?"

He nodded. "Skippy couldn't do it as good as me. He was better at hearing people and speaking to them. I can speak in people's heads, make them do stuff."

"Wowsers."

"It comes in handy."

"I see that." In ten minutes I had learned more about this ungodly ability than I had my entire life. I'm not sure how much of it was applicable, but eagerly, I soaked it up, hoping to be better armed.

"What are your gifts? Tell me your story."

"I see ghosts," I whispered. "They step out of people, they do stuff. Sometimes I hear them mumbling, but I can't really make out the words."

"More than just yourself?" Edward swiped he bottle from my hand and took a swig. "That's wild, are they here now?"

I shook my head. "They do their own thing. They don't listen to me. I thought they were devils."

"We have that in common," he said. "At first, I believed it was God speaking to me. I haven't decided if I was disappointed when I discovered it was the baker in the building next to where I slept."

"Can you read my thoughts?"

"Only sometimes, and only when you scream them at me. It's harder to read the minds of people like us."

He pulled his hand off the bar and dangled it by my thigh, palms up. "You're going to feel a tugging sensation. It'll be slight, but throw your mind at it."

"What?" I lowered my hand, hovering just above his.

He grabbed my hand, locking his fingers with mine as you would a lover. "Trust me," the words spread through my head, a warm, inviting sensation.

How does one throw their thoughts? Or run toward a sensation? The tugging he described was more like a whisper beckoning me to follow, weak, timid, and distant. I imagined chasing the voice, hurling myself in its direction.

I stood in a white room. No, not a room. There were no walls, no floor, no ceiling. Nothing simply stretched for eternity. The abundance of light should have forced me to squint, but my eyes acted as if it were no more than a bedside lamp. The dress I wore to the herbal shop was gone, and I was left standing in a pair of trousers and a powder-blue blouse.

"What in God's name?"

"Don't be scared." I spun about to see Edward wearing a tailored suit. The man from the bar had transformed from a wretch into a gentleman. His hair was tightly cropped to his head, and it looked as if a barber had just scraped the stubble from his face.

"What the hell is this?"

"Skippy called it the white room. It's like a secret clubhouse for people with our abilities. It can feel as if minutes or even hours have passed here, but our bodies may have only blinked once or twice."

"Our bodies? What in the hell is happening?" I'll admit, I wasn't exactly handling this as well as I hoped. A second ago, I sat in Harry's dingy bar, basking in the smell of stale beer. Now, within the blink of an eye, I wore fresh clothes and stood in something out of a horror novel.

"This is your mind and my mind meeting in a neutral place. It's like a playground for our kind. Your thoughts are what matter here. Your body is still in the pub."

The room transformed, a replica of the bar faded into sight. I watched as we came into view, still sitting at the counter, our hands grasped away from prying eyes. Harry and the other patrons were gone. All that remained were Edward and I. I didn't understand it. It wasn't even worth trying.

"You keep saying our kind. What is our kind?"

Edward stood shoulder-to-shoulder with me, appreciating his handiwork. There was a grin stretched across his face. I watched his hand squeeze mine tighter, and somewhere far, far away, I swore I could feel the sensation.

"We're mentalists, 'Nore."

Chapter Thirteen

Edward's words repeated in my head. We had exchanged pleas-
antries, and he promised to call to check up the next day. The pickpocket had done something nobody else could. With a simple
phrase, he gave a label to a part of me I had thought broken. He said
it with admiration, a smile stapled across his face. For a moment, the
ghosts didn't seem so daunting.

"A mentalist," I whispered just loud enough to break the silence
in my bedroom.

The day had been long, and it was hard keeping track of so many
minor adventures. I had forgotten about Claudette and the satchel,
or my intent on finding a serial killer stalking the streets of New
York. Edward had brought my world to a screeching halt, making
me forget my honey-do list as he revealed parts of me I didn't know
existed.

"Oh, that smells just awful," Eleanor said sniffing the liquid. The
tea had been steeping for the last ten minutes. Susan Lee had gone to
bed as soon as I got home, giving me a quick inspection before retir-
ing. She wanted to make sure I wasn't staying out after curfew and
that I didn't have a gash decorating my neck.

I dimmed the lights in my room until it approached pitch black.
Eying the cup, I wondered what Claudette had slipped into the linen

pouch. For some strange reason, I trusted the woman. I'm sure in the morning I'd blame my sudden fondness of strangers on a desperate need to understand the ghosts.

"Bottoms up." I lifted the cup, the steam starting to settle. Holding my breath, I drank the vile liquid. I didn't stop until the teabag smacked against my lips. What did I expect? The safest place was at home in bed with a nurse sleeping in the room next to mine as I started this journey.

"I'm out of my mind." Edward had been sure of himself, more than able to handle a crisis. He owned his telepathy and made it work for him. No part of him feared the unique gifts he had at his disposal. I hated admitting it, but I was jealous.

If I had control, even a little, my life would be different. I could be working the farm, my father might still be alive. Perhaps I'd be living in a house just down the road from him. The family would meet for Sunday meals prepared by Momma. Benjie would arrive with his fiancé, and we'd sit down to eat while Momma made nosey inquiries about when she'd become a grandma.

The patchwork quilt on my bed was cool to the touch as I got cozy. Before I knew it, a yawn escaped, and I contemplated crawling under the covers and calling it a night. It had been a busy day, and my body fought to fall asleep before the tea had a chance to take effect.

I wondered what it would be like if the ghosts listened, or if I could see multiple futures. Having a choice, being able to shape my own destiny meant freedom. I wanted that. I wanted it so much that even the possibility had me daydreaming about the future. What new wonderments would open themselves to me? Or how might I improve the world if I knew dangers before they turned into a reality?

My ghost sat facing me at the end of the bed, legs crossed as she breathed in through her nose and out through her mouth. I had spent hours in that position, trying to calm myself when the ghosts tormented me. The hospital had attempted to teach us to meditate when our emotions were out of control. The ghost blinked out of existence, and I nearly gasped at the figure that returned.

I rolled out of bed and backed away from the thing meditating in my place. Green skin covered the woman as she held a similar pose to my ghost. From her back, massive wings stretched outward, draped along the bedroom floor. She focused on her breathing. Not a muscle in her body moved.

I often claimed the ghosts were demons, but this was the first time they had taken on the appearance of the devil himself. Her eyes opened and, for a moment, I thought she could see me. Our eyes locked, and a gasp slipped out at the sight of yellow irises glowing between blinks. I nearly fell backward when she stood upright, her head partially penetrating the ceiling of my room.

"What are you?" I whispered.

The woman ran through the air, vanishing through the wall into the next room. I followed, flinging the door open to see the kitchen vanished, replaced by an aerial view of New York City. Just over the threshold between the rooms, the floor ended, towering straight down for at least twenty stories. I took a step back, a damp, cool breeze blowing through the doorway.

I looked over my shoulder in preparation for hiding under my covers. What the hell? On the bed, a duplicate of myself nuzzled a pillow, turning slightly in response to the chill. I held up my hands to see if I was real.

Daring to look through the door to the city below, I found a dark alleyway had replaced it. I stepped through, testing the cement on the other side with my big toe. Putting my weight on the foot, I appeared in a long alley running between two buildings. The ground was wet and cold, the aftermath of a horrid downpour.

"Where am I?" I asked. I wanted to make sure I was still in the bed, but when I turned around, red bricks had replaced the doorway. They had blocked any return home, leaving me to fend for myself in this alternate reality.

The sun had long since set, casting the alley in a darkness that made it difficult to see the bags of trash or trashcans scattered along the wall. My eyes fought to adjust and make sense of the shadows. I put my hands in front of me, feeling around for anything I might trip over.

There was no time to panic, nor to sort out how I just went from the safety of my bedroom to an alley somewhere in the streets of

New York. I had seen a woman with wings, and I couldn't figure out if my twin lying in bed was a ghost? Maybe I was the ghost? I needed to get out of here and find safety, perhaps to Claudette's so I could ask what had been in that concoction.

The teabag. Claudette had said it would help, but I didn't expect a vision quest. Normally when I saw flashes of the future, they were quick glimpses. I imagined them through a window, and as quickly as they appeared, they'd vanish. This was the first time I partook in the vision itself.

The sound of boxes falling over came from somewhere between the mouth of the alley and my unfortunate location. "Hello?" I didn't dare move closer to the exit. Instead, I lowered myself, shrinking behind what I thought might be trashcans.

A figure stepped out of the shadows close to the street. I couldn't make out if they were male or female, but I caught the reflection of something shiny in their hands. It only took a moment before I realized they held a straightedge razor.

The man charged out of the alley toward an unsuspecting gentleman. I yelled, hoping either would turn to see me. I ditched my hiding spot, chasing the assailant. The victim struggled, trying to punch the attacker. I jumped through the air, determined to drag the man with the blade to the sidewalk.

I sailed through the image, landing on the pavement. Spring to my feet, I stopped cold in my tracks. The man being attacked could be any New Yorker, a white t-shirt with suspenders, and dark-colored trousers. The attacker, however, he sent a chill through my body. A smile stretched across his face didn't match the ferocity of his grip on the man's coat.

"Stop," I heard the word clear as day. The attacker didn't let go. The man repeated himself. "Stop, I said." I found the statement awkward. In the clutches of death, he believed a single phrase capable of halting the man's attack.

The victim grabbed the attacker's bomber jacket, bringing his forehead into the man's face. The scene slowed as a ghost of the attacker staggered backward from its owner. There were several ghosts, each of them holding a slightly different pose. I saw hundreds of versions, each decision in the upcoming fight spelled out. If I followed one path, I could see the ending, the killer's blade dragging across his victim's throat.

I followed the variations, each resulting in the same manner. Spikes exploded in my head before I could follow any further. I watched as the man in the bomber jacket lunged, sidestepping his victim and spinning about. He had his arm around the man's chest, preventing him from fighting back. The blade flashed, and I looked on in horror as a razor dragged across the victim's neck.

I couldn't do anything but observe while the man bled to death. He tried to hold in the liquid, pressing his palms firmly against his skin, but to no avail. As the attacker pulled his victim into the alley, the grotesque smile persisted, sprawled across his face as he hid his handiwork.

The blackness from the shadows consumed the street until all I could see was the dead man. I didn't know when it was going to happen. It could be five minutes from now or five days. But like all my other predictions, it was a truth waiting to unfold.

The scene faded, and I stood inside Claudette's shop. It was sterile, the scent of fresh herbs completely absent. I tried to remember the smell, the aroma of freshly cut flowers, herbs, and things I never admired before. The visions rarely let me experience any of my other senses. Trying to concentrate and recall each of the scents from the jars lining the shelves.

Was this part of learning to expand these gifts? Was there more than watching untimely demises? I wished Claudette would arrive and step through that curtain so I could bombard her with a thousand questions. Was this the result of the tea? Was this because of what Edward told me? She had been kind and offered me advice without anything in return.

A chalk outline rose from the floor. I waited for the scene to transition to another alley, to see a dead body, but the room remained. The sun poured through the windows, high in the sky. I tried searching for a clock, a newspaper, any indication of the time.

As I charged for the backroom, the cool sensation of my blanket enveloped my body. The pressure of my pillow pressed against the back of my head, bringing me out of the shop and back to my bed. I blinked several times, before jolting upright. I shimmied to the edge, looking for my ghostly doppelgänger, but I was alone.

Three futures, three very distinct timelines. Now I had to sort through them and make sense of the images before they came to pass.

Resting on my nightstand, a beautiful hardbound book filled with empty pages. Frank had always urged me to express myself, to try and cope with these terrible things. For the first time, I recorded my visions.

Dear Diary…

Chapter Fourteen

The ghosts seldom went away.

Momma had taken to shushing me whenever I asked about the ghosts walking around the house. Sitting in the kitchen, the white things fluttered about, acting like Momma or Poppa, or even Benjie from time to time. When my eyes grew distant, she'd thwap me on the hand with her wooden spoon.

"We'll have none of the devil's work in my home," she said.

I focused on the pie she was making, humming quietly as she went about throwing flour on what would become the crust. She wanted to celebrate Poppa being home, and the best way she knew was with her cooking. I got to eat the peelings, sucking the juice out of them first before chewing on them.

"When will they be home?"

"Ellie, asking the same question over and over won't change my answer. You need to learn some patience, little lady. Your dad will be back from the hardware store when he's done."

There were no more peels, the last one tickling my throat as I swallowed. I was about to ask Momma to play when the bang of Robinson's truck signaled Poppa's return. Running through the house, I ignored Momma yelling for me to be careful. I was out the screen door and on the front porch in the blink of an eye.

No Poppa. I spun about, annoyed. Ghosts. I didn't jump, but I gulped when I saw him sitting on the swing. He held his arm over the shoulders of a smaller ghost, a girl. It was the first time I had seen my ghost. I shook my head, wiping my eyes, seeing if they'd go away. It never worked.

Bang. Distracted from the ghost, I watched the dirt cloud flying into the air down the road. Robinson's truck approached quickly, leaving a trail of brown dust stretching behind it. I climbed down the stairs, careful to avoid the tiny rocks in the pathway.

The truck roared toward the house, only slowing when it approached the front yard. Poppa helped Benjie out of the back and then jumped down after him. He grabbed two bags full of stuff. I didn't want to ask, but I hoped he had gotten watermelon for dinner. He always brought watermelon home when he went into town without Momma.

It irked me that Benjie got to go with Poppa while I had to sit at home and help Momma in the kitchen. I hated cooking. I wanted to get my hands dirty and build things. Poppa had promised we'd make a tree fort together when he got back, I would have to ask him when we could start.

"Benjie, go on inside and wash up for dinner." The booger took one of the bags and waddled up the steps. He nearly dropped the bag while he tried to open the screen.

Poppa walked up to me, ruffling my hair so it fell out of the braids Momma insisted I wear. He set his bag down near the door, signaling me to come sit with him on the porch swing. We had spent plenty of evenings sitting on the front porch while he read *The Wonderful Wizard of Oz* to me. The serious expression on his face made me nervous. Poppa was never grumpy with me. I brushed the dirt off my dress, straightening it along my butt as I sat next to him.

"We need to have a talk, you and I."

"I didn't do anything wrong."

When Poppa smiled, the tiny lines around his eyes got darker, making him look a little older. He shook his head slowly. "You're not in trouble, Ellie. But I think it's time we had a heart-to-heart."

"What's wrong?"

Before he responded, I knew what this conversation was going to be about. I had butterflies in my tummy and was worried Momma would get mad if she found out I was talking about *them*. She demanded I not talk about the ghosts, that it was opening the door for the devil to enter her home.

"Are you still seeing them?"

I nodded.

He kicked off, making the swing rock back and forth. He took his time as he thought of what to say. I don't know why, but I started crying. Scary things were happening and nobody believed me when I told them. Momma forbid me to talk about it, and Benjie made-up a rhyme about me being crazy. I didn't want to be different. I didn't want my father to see me hysterical.

"It's okay, Ellie." He wrapped his arm over my shoulders and pulled me close. "The first day I got back, Benjie asked how you knew I was coming home."

I might not remember where I left my Sunday shoes, but I remembered the day Poppa came home. "The ghost. He stood on the porch. He looked just like you. Then you were home."

"Do the ghosts always look like me?"

I shook my head. "Sometimes Momma and Benjie too."

"Do they always show you things before they happen?"

It had only been minutes since I saw a ghost of Poppa sitting in the same place, his arm hugging me. They didn't always show me things, but more often than not, they did. "Sometimes. I saw a ghost of you hugging me while we talked."

"Right now?"

I nodded.

"Anything else?"

I wiped my nose on the back of my sleeve as I sat up straight. "You believe me? Nobody..."

"Shhh," he held a finger to his mouth, "this is our secret. I don't want you scaring your mother, or Benjie for that matter. But I believe you."

He believed me? Something on my face caused him to kiss my forehead. He spoke in his church voice. "I've seen things I can't explain. Maybe you can see things too. You wouldn't lie."

I shook my head, ready to cry again. I wrapped my arms around his wide chest and he patted me on the back while we rocked together. We sat like that for the next bit until I finally stopped crying. Each time the breeze picked up, we listened to the rustling of the wheat, something we hadn't done in ages.

"I was gone for a long time… I missed you, punkin."

"I missed you too."

Chapter Fifteen

"It's not safe for you out there," I said.

"I'm not the one who vanishes all day and comes waltzing in all hours of the night." Susan Lee had a point.

She had her arms wrapped around her chest, tightly hugging herself. Her robe was pulled tight with hair drawn back in large curlers. For a change, I woke before her, putting on the kettle to prepare coffee. I might not be the best roommate, but I had my moments.

The radio had run the serial killer story once already, returning to news of the war. Susan Lee had only caught the tail end. Another murder had taken place, this time a man dragged into an alley and slaughtered. I didn't need to hear to know the specifics. I had lived them.

My diary sat on my nightstand, echoing the reporter almost word-for-word. My account held far more details, the man's clothes, his determination to fight back, his insistence that the attacker stop. Even as I wrote into the late hours of the night, I knew there was something about the vision I missed, a key moment that would break the case wide open.

"I called Frank," Susan Lee admitted. "He will have one of the men drop by the hospital when my shift is over."

I gave her a hug, an act so unlike me she almost jumped. I pulled back and sat down at the table. She huffed as she joined me.

"The women at the volunteer center will miss me. I don't like not being able to help with the war, Eleanor. Those men need our support."

For all my visions of the future, never had I seen the end of the conflict. Yes, I knew when Hitler died, but did it continue in his absence? I imagined it continued for at least another decade. The way the news reported, it sounded as if victory was imminent, but it came across as propaganda. America had fallen into a pit of despair, but not Susan Lee. This woman single-handedly lifted the spirits of those around her. Her optimism might be naïve, but it was a welcomed change of pace for me.

"I am free today. What if I get the paper to write the boys letters for moral support? I can buy you some yarn for socks?"

"You're going to join?"

"Yes," I said, quite proud of my sudden willingness to make our little part of the world a better place. "In fact, I am. And you know what, I bet we can go even further."

"Who are you? What have you done with Eleanor? Should I check your temperature?"

"Stop it, you ninny," I laughed. "It's official, alert the world, Susan Lee has turned me into an optimist!"

Susan Lee's yelped as I stood, lifting my cup of coffee into the air. "Susan Lee, nurse, defender of the sick, and supporter of the brave has officially changed my heart."

She giggled, the worry fading away from her face. She snatched her coffee, taking a quick sip so as not to spill the precious liquid. Raising it to meet mine, she let the porcelain make a slight clinking noise.

"Now, Eleanor Bouvier, how do you think we can do better? Will you have us enlisting in the army? Are we going to single-handedly win the war?"

"Hitler wouldn't stand a chance!"

I hadn't thought about it before, about how I could affect mankind on a grander scale. Susan Lee was unaware of my secrets, but she made me question what I was doing with myself. I had no doubt she would change the world, but what about me? It might be time to be more like the ever-optimistic Susan Lee.

"So what are we going to do then, knit socks for the entire army?"

"To do that, we'll need an army," I said. Her face turned sour. It was an expression saved for when I boasted some grand idea she would detest. I had seen it plenty since we lived together, making me thankful she offered unconditional love. If there were conditions, we might not have lasted this long.

"The gym," I said, returning to my seat to have a sip of coffee. "Frank's buddies are veterans. His support group is all veterans. What if we recruit an army, most of them would return to the war if they could? I'm certain, with a little Susan Lee pep talk, they'd be knitting socks and rolling bandages like a factory line."

She didn't speak, instead lowering herself to the chair while she gently blew at the steam coming off her coffee. There was a mulling over the idea, a slight bobbing of her head as she ran through the pros and cons.

"Can they knit?"

"No," I admitted, "but I remember a woman who taught her bumbling roommate how to knit."

It was a slow transition. Her lips relaxed from their pursed position, the edges turning up. The smile grew. I didn't have to hear her thoughts to know she imagined a group of burly men with knitting needles telling stories while they worked.

"What brought about this change of heart?" Her optimism maintained a bit of suspicion.

"Just thinking about the future," I confessed. "It's filled with a thousand possibilities, and I think for the first time, I'm seeing where I belong in it."

Saying it out loud pushed away terrors of my past. The ghosts didn't seem quite so scary. No, they weren't demons determined to destroy me, they were an opportunity to be something great. These thoughts were so foreign I almost forgot the sensation, the very word for the warmth spreading through my body.

Hope. Once again, Susan Lee scored a victory.

"I don't want you getting hurt," I said, holding my hand to Frank's chest, stopping him from passing me. "One of us has powers, the other doesn't."

"The other has a gun." Frank reached inside the breast of his jacket. He gave the weapon a light pat. I should have guessed. Frank could brawl with the best of them, but he wouldn't take chances with my safety.

"I guess I didn't think that far ahead." Even I had to frown at the irony of the statement. My determination to change the world might be well intentioned, but I wasn't seeing the big picture clearly. Thankfully, Frank filled in the gaps.

"Do you think the killer is going after this woman?" The moment I mentioned the vision over the phone, he had asked for an address. I thought about calling Edward, but I didn't want him to know about the visions. Right now, Frank was the only man I trusted with the entire truth. It also happened he was more than capable of handling himself in a fight.

"I saw a chalk outline like at the murder scene. I don't know if it's specific to Claudette, but I can't risk losing her."

Frank had spent long nights in my youth, holding me while I screamed in my sleep. He didn't understand what was happening to me, but he did his best to maintain my sanity. Claudette might have answers, and to this amazing man, it meant she was worth saving. He'd be more than willing to put his life in jeopardy to protect my future. It was chivalrous, but that same determination worried me.

"Stay behind me, Frank. I've got this."

There was no bravado, no chauvinistic attitude originating from his penis. One thing that made Frank amazing was his willingness to let a woman take the lead. When the killer was in jail and the city returned to its own version of normal, we'd find him a wife.

He followed me down the alley until we stood at the entrance to Claudette's shop. The sign read "Closed." Too early to be open. I reached for the door and noticed broken wood around the lock. I feared we were too late.

"Claudette," I shouted as I threw the door wide.

It was him—the killer in the bomber jacket. Claudette remained frozen in the doorway leading to the back of her shop. The man had a razor in his hand, ready to charge at them. His head turned slowly, cocked to one side as he sized me up. I wasn't intimidating, despite my ability to throw a mean punch, I was still a small and weaponless woman.

"Claudette, get back," I called out.

"Eleanor, move," Frank shouted.

The killer stepped forward slightly, putting me between him and Frank. He ran toward me, his knife hand drawn back, ready to end the encounter in one fell swoop. Frank pulled at my jacket, yanking me out of reach of the killer.

The force of the gunshot left my ears ringing. The man spun about as the shot landed just below his shoulder. He carried the momentum forward, kicking at Frank's outstretched hand, slamming the gun against the wall. The blade followed, a swipe downward, inches from my face, slicing into Frank's arm.

Frank cursed, tossing me back into the alley. The man snapped another kick forward, striking Frank in the chest, knocking him off his feet. The attacker wasn't a formal boxer or a scrappy brawler. Each movement was specific, direct, calculated.

"Child, the ghosts," Claudette yelled.

They answered her call like a long-lost friend. Frank's ghost had him pushing away from the attack, frantically kicking to put space between them. Even Claudette's ghost stood in the shop, watching the fray through the broken door.

It was the ghost stepping out of the attacker that interested me. The number of specters multiplied, the creepy smile repeating until there were a dozen versions of the killer. The ghosts showed me multiple futures. I couldn't tell which was the truth. I'd never been able to sort through them fast enough to win the fight. With so many moving specters, I found it hard to concentrate on the man. My one advantage turned into a mass of confusion.

The man's arm moved in slow motion as he raised the razor, slowing until it came to a stop. My ghost stepped out of my body. It danced with the attacker's ghost swiping left, arms blocking, but leaving a gash through my jacket. Reset. The attacker shouldered into my ghost, sending it tumbling to the alley. Reset. My ghost stepped in, gripping the wrist, slamming it against the wall until it dropped.

I followed. We replaced our ghosts, and I worked inside his reach, my left hand grabbing his wrist, shoving hard, smacking it against the brick. The razor clanked to the floor at the same time his other hand wrapped around my neck. My ghost drove the palm of its hand into the crook of his elbow, forcing him to drop me. I did the same.

Our ghosts struggled against one another. He'd throw up a knee as he grabbed me by the hair, driving me downward. I didn't need to see destiny. I needed choices, the strikes and dodges that would lead me to victory.

He grabbed me by the back of the head and I blocked his rising knee, preventing him from crushing my nose. The ghost wasn't right, a single blow had changed. I punched forward, striking him in the groin. He flung me to the side, the punch to his manhood doing nothing to slow him. An attacker who didn't flinch when struck in his manhood. There *was* something different about him.

He picked up his razor, flipping open the blade. The glint of steel and the perpetual glee on his face made him terrifying, more so in the light. The count of ghosts exploded, dozens of him, Frank, and myself. I found it almost impossible to work my way through each scenario. There were choices, and each choice led to another dozen ghosts. I watched as each action and consequence created a new future. Only one ended well, not perfect, but well.

He stood over me, his legs on each side of my torso. I prepared for the sting, the sharp pain shooting through my bicep. The swipe of the blade fell short of my face, dragging across my jacket, cutting through the fabric and into my flesh. I shoved my right leg between us, to stop him from reaching my arm again.

It barely slowed him, but it gave Frank time to land a punch. Knuckles drove into the killer's jaw. Spit and blood splattered along the pavement. It wouldn't—

The gun fired, a hole blowing through the man's upper arm, sending jacket stuffing and gore raining down on my face. He let go of the blade while Frank jumped backward, unsure of who was shooting.

The attacker didn't make a sound, no groan, no howl. He charged down the alley, running more quickly than I'd expect a man with two bullet holes in him to move.

Claudette stood in the doorway, the weapon shaking between her hands. She fell to her knees, her face frozen in a state of shock. The gun rattled on the floor as she dropped it. It wasn't a victory, we didn't catch the killer, but it had been the only future where all three of us walked away alive.

Did I change the future, or is this how it was always meant to be? At the moment, I couldn't tell. I hurt, Frank hurt, even Claudette hurt. We weren't doing well as crime fighters, but at least we were alive to recount the tale.

Chapter Sixteen

I hissed loudly. The gash cut deep enough I thought it'd need stitches, but Claudette swore she had alternatives. The salve she applied was clear with a slight green tint. I had no idea what she was rubbing over the open wound, but it hurt. When she finished applying it, she rolled a bandage around my arm.

"It will heal quickly, and you shouldn't have much of a scar, child."

She poured more of the liquid on her hand, warming it as she rubbed them together. When Frank resisted, she grabbed his arm and laid it out on the table. Ignoring the blood covering him, she massaged the ointment into his skin. It made me feel braver when he hissed.

"Do you know who that was?" The man's twisted smile remained burnt into my brain. I couldn't get the image out of my mind.

"No," she said as she pulled her hands away from Frank. He left his arm lying on the table in the middle of the shop as she prepared another roll of bandages. "I have never seen that thing before."

"Ouch," he said.

"Stop moving," Claudette insisted. She finished wrapping his arm and tucked the end so it wouldn't loosen. She grabbed a towel, wiping her hands clean of the goop.

"You said 'thing', not man." Claudette struck me as a woman who chose her words carefully.

"Yes." She started putting away her jars filled with herbs. "Did you see that face? There was nothing there. There was nothing human in him, just a thing."

"He didn't flinch when I punched him."

"Or when I did," Frank added.

"Not a man, a thing. Not a he, an it," Claudette corrected.

As she pulled apart the semantics of our conversation, I hovered over the spot where I had seen the chalk drawing. I wanted to cheer that we changed the future, but without a time frame, it was possible Claudette might still die in another attempt.

"Why did it want you?" I couldn't help but stare at where the white lines had seeped up through the floor in my vision. Reaching down, I ran my hand along the memory, hoping it would spark something. I needed the ghosts right now. They were the answer to this problem, but like always, they only showed themselves when *they* wanted.

"What did you see, child?"

"I made the tea." I watched as Frank's face went cold at the admission. His support group was about breaking the hold of alcohol. I knew he wouldn't like me using unknown drugs to wrangle the ghosts.

"I saw a woman with wings, she was..." I had to think about how otherworldly the female demon had been. "She was terrifying. But my guess is she had nothing to do with this. She struck me as peaceful. There was the man who died this morning. I watched it happen. That *thing* attacked him. He fought back, but he didn't stand a chance. It slit his throat and dragged him into an alley like the others."

"That's not what has you crawling around my floor, child. What did you see?"

I stood, brushing the invisible chalk from my hands. I wasn't sure how to phrase it. How do you explain to a person you'd seen their demise? It happened in flashes for so many, but to reveal their doomsday clock measured in days instead of years? It was awkward at best.

"Was it me? Is that what the visions showed you?"

I didn't want to be the one to tell her. The weight in the pit of my stomach grew. I feared I might hurl. I hadn't spoken of a person's death since my father. Shaking my head, I fought against the memories.

"You saw my death?" Claudette didn't sound shocked at the idea. "Child, I have led a wonderful life and seen things I could never imagine. If fate has decided it's time, I welcome the chance to embrace my ancestors."

"It wasn't you exactly, just the chalk outline they use in murder scenes. But the future might have changed."

Claudette barreled through the lie. "Has it before?"

"No." The pat on the back from Frank was well intentioned, but I felt like a child again.

"Death comes for us all." The smile on her face remained out of place as we talked about her inevitable demise. "It's part of the journey."

"How do you know all of this?" Frank didn't pull his hand away. I couldn't tell if he kept it there to comfort me or to remind himself that the conversation about ghosts and the future wasn't coming from mad women.

"My family has their own gifts. The women have always been able to sense the angels, or ghosts as Eleanor calls them. They showed my mother the world as it was, things she couldn't possibly know. It lasted well into her twenties, one of the oldest."

"Frank…"

"Eleanor tried to do that when she went to the crime scene, to see the past, I mean."

"Maybe she can, but the Loa have blessed each of us differently. My mother could see things long since passed, I could not. But I could feel it. Every object endured an emotional journey, some stronger than others. Often, a ring or a favorite book could move me to tears."

Edward had said the same thing. He and his mentor had similar abilities that worked ever so slightly different. Claudette's family shared the curse, but each held their own variation. Edward hadn't lied.

"What about now?" I asked.

"As I became a woman, the gift of the Loa faded until the ti-bon-ange stopped speaking directly to me."

"And your mother?"

I tried not to be eager as she opened up to us about her family. The moment I asked, I regretted it. The smile that persevered even as she discussed her own mortality slipped. She cleared her throat, eyes cast downward.

"The Loa are powerful, and if their gifts persist, it can be more than a mortal is capable of enduring."

Death. She didn't have to say it, I knew exactly what she meant. I had stared death in the face more than I cared to remember. We differed on calling this a gift, but I understood the desire to escape the constant barrage. I considered myself stronger now, but I frequently wondered if there'd come a day I wouldn't be able to resist.

"We're sorry," Frank said.

"It's part of life. Some live cautiously looking for length, others live their lives hard seeking fullness. My mother lived to the fullest." She stared at me. She said she couldn't see the angels, but she remained fixated on me, as if she knew she spoke my truth. They may not speak directly, but I suspected they whispered.

"Why you? Why did it want you?" I asked.

"Us," she said.

"Us?" I gulped.

"It chose me until you arrived. It didn't care for your friend."

"Frank," he said, giving a slight nod.

"Once Frank was out of the way, it wanted you. Now what might we have in common?"

"He's a pervert." Frank, bless his heart, tried.

I rolled my eyes. "You're dense. It's because we're women. He killed men already..." I trailed off as I thought about it.

"He is seeking those the Loa speak through."

"How can you be sure?" Frank asked. He was right. That was a huge jump, considering how many deaths had occurred. Did this mean every victim had been…

"They're like us. They're *all* like us," I whispered. "The man in my vision, he tried to make it stop. He spoke the words, but it didn't work. I've seen the trick before." The light went on. "He attempted to influence it."

"Influence it?" Asked Frank.

"Eleanor is learning about the Loa's blessings." Claudette touched my cheek, cupping my face in her hands. "I am sorry it has taken us this long to meet, child. I had my mother, and she her own mother. Frank has seen you this far, but you need to learn to harness these gifts. You require a mentor."

She reached down and clutched my hands tightly. Her expression softened at the sight of Frank's disgruntled, furrowed brow. "You are also welcome on this journey. It is important that her caretaker understand what is happening. This is not a solitary venture."

"Oh," he said. His jealousy was cute, but her ability to disarm him, that was short of supernatural.

"Thank you, Claudette. I would like that very much."

"Now be gone, you two." Her back straightened while she scanned the room. "They have violated my sanctuary. It will need purifying before the Lao bless my medicines."

"I will be back," I assured her.

"I do not need to see the future to know this is the truth." What if Claudette entered my life ten years ago? All the time spent in dread and self-loathing, all sidestepped by the willingness of a single woman to guide me. My heart ached as her hand slipped from mine.

Frank walked from the shop and I followed close behind. Lagging, I watched as he slid the gun into his shoulder holster. I turned my hand over, revealing the small piece of paper snuck to me by Claudette. I unfolded it as Frank stepped onto the street.

"Danger."

Frank escorted me to the door of my apartment. He'd been quiet for most of the walk, stewing in his own thoughts. I let him. The man had strapped a gun to his chest and followed me to a strange woman's store to help stop a killer. I couldn't think of anybody who I'd rather have at my back. At the same time, the tiny sheet of paper in my pocket left me wondering if the danger was from Frank, or to him.

"What's wrong?"

"It's not worth worrying about," he replied.

"No secrets, Frank. Something's on your mind."

That half-cocked grin he managed while he worked through his thoughts was just another on the list of endearing traits. First, I stop a killer, then I learn to change the future. Then I find him a wife. I almost laughed at the thought. The wife would easily be the most difficult of the three.

"It's been you and me for a long time. It's just..." he paused as he searched for the word, "different. Give me a little time to adjust."

"Frank, you and I—"

"Oh no, not that. You and me will always be you and me. It's more that I've been the expert in all things, Eleanor. Now you have a boyfriend and a," he smirked at the thought, "a mentor who knows all about this stuff."

"Edward isn't my boyfriend. And Claudette will never be an expert in all things 'Eleanor.' They only know what they need. You're the only person I trust with all the pieces."

He opened his arms. "Give the old man a hug." He was careful to never say, "your old man." His respect for Poppa held no bounds. I wrapped my arms around his chest, mindful not to bump the gun. I barely remembered my father, and it had been years since I could recall his face with any certainty. My father died a hero, and he ensured I had a second father in place before he surrendered.

"You'll always be the only old man for me." That made him squeeze tighter. No, no matter what Claudette might think, he would never be a source of danger in my life.

"Did I mention that I volunteered the guys at the gym to knit socks for the soldiers? I might have also said your group would be interested."

"Eleanor," he pulled away with a scowl. "Those men don't knit."

"That's good, Susan Lee would be mad if she didn't have students to teach. If she can't, they can always roll bandages."

He shook his head. "I'll talk to them. But I have a feeling you'll be boxing a lot of men to win this bet."

"I'm not convincing them!" I raised my voice as if he offended my sensibilities. "They're going against Susan Lee. They'll never stand a chance."

"No, no, they won't," he laughed. "I'll pitch the idea today. But I'm only doing it so I don't have to face the wrath of that woman."

A minute later, I was in the building and fidgeting with the keys to the door. Out of habit, I checked the pad of paper next to the phone. Susan Lee had scribbled that she'd be home late with a note, "One of the doctors offered to escort me." Beneath that was the name "Edward" with a time and a corner of the park. I couldn't help but laugh at the dozen hearts bubbling out of his name. The woman's persistence was undeniable.

I checked the clock, making sure I had enough time to shower and even more to hide the bruising. The sucker punch to the face was just starting to fade, but I'm sure my ribcage would be sore from smacking against the street. I had to pause at the thought of dolling myself up for Edward.

"Is this a date?" I asked myself.

I disrobed quickly and stared at myself in the bedroom mirror. Pulling the pins from my hair, it fell on my shoulders, the curls refusing to unwind. The right side of my ribcage was red, but I think I'd be lucky enough to escape bruising. However, the bandages on my arm would be a bit harder to conceal. I let out a low whistle. I wasn't half bad to look at in the nude.

"Not that you will see it, Edward."

The shower proved difficult, my arm hanging out of the curtain, trying to keep my bandages dry. The water cooled before I had a chance to rinse the soap from my hair. Normally I'd be in and out before it could turn cold. The moment it got chilly, I had an image of the ice bath at the hospital. A tightness clutched at my chest, making it hard to breathe. I spun the knob, shivering.

For the first few weeks, I avoided the shower, terrified of the sound and sensation of water on my skin. Even when I dared, I never stayed long enough for my fingers to prune. There are some horrors etched into my psyche I couldn't outrun.

The memories returned. If I concentrated hard enough, jagged cubes of ice dug into my skin. It hurt until I went numb enough not to care. There was no point in resisting. If I fought, the orderlies would hold me down like a beast. I didn't want the ghosts, I wanted them gone. I entered the ice bath willingly, more than ready to endure pain to be free of the devil.

Eleanor.

Edward's voice echoed through my head. I realized I had been standing in the shower long enough for the water to vanish through the drain. Despite the warm day outside, tiny bumps had raised on my arms as I hugged myself.

I sensed… are you all right?

I'm fine. It was a lie. Could he tell otherwise? I still didn't know just how invasive his powers were.

Good.

"You're okay," I said out loud, trying to distance myself from the past. If I had my way, I would never think about that place again. A decade had shown me that there were worse things than ghosts. I needed to get dressed and head out if I was going to meet Edward in the park.

Chapter Seventeen

The truck engine roared as it came speeding down the road. It made an awful grinding noise as it approached the house. Clouds of dust would normally fill the air, but it had rained earlier in the day and it was too dark to see.

"Ellie, is this him?"

Poppa believed.

I nodded quickly. He ruffled my hair as he stood up. With a pat on the shoulder, he pointed to the door. "Go inside, like we talked about. If Momma or Benjie try to come out, tell them he has a gun."

Last night I had a dream. I saw the old pickup truck going back and forth on the road, and then a man older than Poppa got out. I couldn't hear what he said, but he was angry. Even in the dark, I could tell he was shouting. When I woke up, I waited until Poppa and I were alone and told him everything. I wasn't sure he believed me then, but he did now.

I opened the screen door just as the truck turned onto the front lawn. Instead of running into the kitchen like I was supposed to, I laid down so I could still see. I didn't know quite what would go on.

Poppa believed the ghosts were showing me things that hadn't happened yet. He asked if I ever thought about the future, and when I shook my head, he had laughed. He said that's good, I was too young to worry about that. I didn't know what he meant, just that I was happy that he didn't claim I was opening the door for the devil.

Poppa stood at the top of the steps, holding his rifle, the end of it pointing at the ground. The motor didn't turn off as the man inside climbed out. He stumbled as he got to the front of the truck. The bottle in his hand fell as he pointed at my father.

"You," the man yelled.

"Jimmy," Poppa replied, "I think it best you get back in your truck and go home."

"I saw you and your son at the store." The man's yelling was hard to understand. His words jumbled together as he shouted. "You and that beautiful baby boy." It sounded like Mr. Jimmy was crying.

"Thanks, Jimmy, but I think it best you go home before Willa misses you."

"I almost came up to say thank you for your service."

In the headlights of the truck, Mr. Jimmy reached into his pants pocket. Poppa raised the rifle, not quite pointing at the man, but enough I knew he worried about what the man might do. He pulled out a sheet of paper, waving it in front of him like we could read it from far away.

"Then I get home and this is in the mailbox."

"Oh, damn." Poppa never swore. "I'm so sorry, Jimmy."

"Save it. Save your pity." The man tried to throw the letter in Poppa's direction, but it caught on the wind, drifting harmlessly to the wet grass.

"Let me drive you home, Jimmy."

"Why! Why did you come back? You survived, why?" The man sounded like a coyote the way he howled. "And my son died."

"Junior is a good man."

"Is? Is! My goddamned son is dead. I'll be lucky if there's a body to put in the ground. His mother's hysterical. You lived. You got to come home. Your boy, you got to see him again."

"Jimm—"

"Save it!" The man reached toward the back of his pants, and Poppa fired his rifle at the ground. He raised the end of the gun and pointed it at Mr. Jimmy.

"Don't do anything you'll regret, Jimmy. I understand you're grieving, but this isn't—"

The man tried to reach behind his back again. Poppa shot his gun and one of the truck's headlights exploded. At this point, I could feel Momma standing over me, looking out the door.

"What in God's good name is going on?"

"Mr. Jimmy's son died."

I don't know why, but that quieted Momma real fast. Benjie stormed down the hallway and she turned around, scooping him up. "Ellie, come to the kitchen right now." I ignored her.

"Don't make me shoot again, Jimmy. You're not taking my kids' dad from them."

Mr. Jimmy slumped against the truck, the sobbing loud enough even I could tell he was crying. He slid down until he was sitting on the grass. I had never seen a grown man cry, let alone wail like the time Benjie broke his finger.

After a minute, Poppa sat down next to Mr. Jimmy, making sure to keep the rifle out of reach. He grabbed something from the man and tossed it in the grass, shiny, but difficult to make out in the dark. He continued crying while Poppa held him. I knew old people sometimes died and went to Heaven, but Mr. Jimmy's son was Poppa's age.

That night Benjie slept in Momma's room, curled up at the foot of the bed like a dog. It had been hours since I went to sleep when Poppa eased the door open. I was having difficulty keeping my eyes from shutting, but I was just too eager to hear what happened. He sat on the edge of my bed while he tucked me in.

"What happened to Mr. Jimmy's son?

"He died," Poppa admitted.

"He's not old."

"No, he's not. He died doing his job trying to protect America."

I had known what Poppa did was dangerous, but this was the first time I thought about the possibility of him dying. "What happened? Why did Mr. Jimmy come here? Why was he so mad at you, Poppa?"

"Sometimes people get sad and confused when bad things

happen. He just needed somebody to listen. He wasn't really angry at me. I think if something happened to Benjie, I'd be the same way."

"Could you have died in the army?"

"Let's not think about that, Ellie. You're special, you know that, right?"

I smiled, his compliment setting aside my worries. "You and Momma always tell us that."

"Not like that," his tone was very serious. "You can see things, Ellie. You were right, those things you see, they're real. They just haven't happened yet."

"Whoa."

"The question is, did it happen that way because you told me? Or would it have happened, anyway?"

I yawned. I was fighting to keep my eyes open. "What do you mean?"

"Nothing." He kissed me on the head. "You're special, Eleanor. Never let anybody tell you different."

"I won't." My eyes shut.

Chapter Eighteen

The storefronts leading to the park were all dark. The owners served overseas, protecting the globe from a man determined to annihilate anybody different from his idea of perfection. Those who remained worked in critical occupations. The women, however, continued to keep America afloat. Filling the workforce, the entertainment industry, even sports, they put on a brave face ushering in a brave world.

Posters hung in the hardware store window. The propaganda ran rampant on both sides, touching upon our fears to increase a sense of civic duty. I knew the outcome of the war, not the details, but the overall victory. It made it difficult to care about it in the here and now, and even more so to keep my mouth shut as people speculated about what might or might not happen.

The image of Rosie with her arm bent, displaying her muscle and unyielding courage always elicited a smile. Women would have a long and hard road ahead of them, but it was a start. They took to manufacturing jobs, proving they were as capable as their husbands and brothers. Her image struck a nerve and the sense of pride made me straighten my shoulders. "We'll get there, missy, not right away, but soon."

I shuffled past the hardware store. At the end of the block, across the street, a lush park interrupted the pavement. New York City was a concrete jungle, so much that people felt the need to create green spaces. They were few and far between, but they were there, hidden behind the towering buildings.

I avoided the path into the park, opting for the feel of soft green grass under my feet. Greens and browns outweighed the gray and red brick. It reminded me of the farm. Momma would yell for me to put on my shoes as I climbed the trees next to the house. The days of playing had long since passed, but as my hand rested on the tree trunk, my fingers remembered.

"Penny for your thoughts," came a voice from behind the tree.

Edward appeared, his hair slicked back, wearing a pair of freshly pressed trousers and suspenders. I had been so caught up in the urgency of meeting another mentalist, I barely had time to admire his handsome features. A toothy grin rested just beneath a slightly crooked nose. Both made him even more charming. I had to remind myself that he was more than an ordinary man. A pickpocket and gambler were words that hovered right behind, dashing and appealing.

"I was remembering as a kid, how I used to climb the trees by our house. Things weren't easier back then, but they were simpler. Sometimes I miss it."

"Not me," he said. "I was in an orphanage for most of my childhood. Life got better once I ran away. I can't imagine it being any better than it is now."

"That sounds horrible." It was a platitude for a person with a complicated past. I didn't want to admit an orphanage would have been preferable over the hospital. Revealing the broken parts was saved for the closest of close friends.

"One day I woke up with a nasty headache and I got to stay home from school." He gave a slight bow, bending his arm for me to accept. I accepted, walking side-by-side with him through the park.

"The headache was bad enough, I thought I might die. Then," he snapped his fingers, "poof, gone. It was as if it had never been there. But it had, and something changed at that moment."

"The voices?"

"I learned that Nuns have incredibly vulgar thoughts!" He escorted me toward a bench overlooking a small pond. "They were nice, but the rules weren't for me. I wanted to be something more than a wretch in their care. As soon as I realized I could hear their thoughts, I ran away."

"My parents are gone now," I didn't need to lie to tell my history. "Frank brought me to New York. He served with my father when I was a girl. He thought the change of scenery might do me some good."

"Did it? Do you some good, I mean?"

He asked a complicated question. When the lies became too complex, be honest. Frank had taught me that in case the ghosts sent me into a fit. "Maybe? I think it's still too soon to decide."

"I love it here." Edward leaned forward, elbows resting on his knees. His eyes fixated on ducks swimming near the edge of the pond. "New York, the only place where you can stand in the open and hide. It's perfect for those like us."

"That sounds lonely."

"They're deaf to the world around them. I can't imagine you'd find it much easier to connect with people like that. Most of the time, I think they'd fall apart if they knew what people around them were thinking. It's too complicated to get close to a person when you can hear their every thought."

The circumstances were slightly different, but I understood what he meant. The last man I allowed to take me out to dinner was not thrilled when I called it quits partway through. Watching him be hit by a car while spinning pasta around my fork left me less than willing to see it to the end. I could sympathize with Edward, but we were indeed unique.

"It's been difficult," I admitted.

"How have you managed? I can't imagine learning about this on my own."

"Honestly? I haven't, not really. I thought I was going crazy. It does what it wants, when it wants. Rarely do I ever have control of it. I didn't think there was a solution. I assumed I was the only one."

He put his hand on mine. "You're not alone. I'll show you how wonderful it can be."

"By picking pockets and liberating wallets from their owners?"

He gave a slight smirk. "It's not my fault they have so much money. They can't keep track of it. And what's a few hundred dollars to those people? They certainly have plenty to spare."

"A regular Robin Hood."

"I like the sound of that," he laughed.

"It means you have to actually give the money to the poor."

Edward jumped up, pulling his pockets free from his trousers. He exaggerated as he shook them. "If I'm not poor, then I don't know who is. Besides, what were you doing at the ball and the boxing match? It looks like I'm not the only one liberating money from the rich."

I laughed at his antics. He returned to the bench, shoving his pockets back into his pants. "So what do you want to know?"

That was *the* question, what did I want to know? I didn't think it could ever be better than seeing horrible things before they happen. In front of me, I have options again. What did I want, I guess I should start at the beginning?

"How do I make it happen? How do you turn it on and off, that thing you did where the mobsters did what you asked?"

"Okay, let's start with the basics. Somewhere inside of you there is this thing, a fire you can say. It's different for all of us, I like to think of a match. By itself, it's just an insignificant piece of wood, but when needed I strike it, I get a little flame. When I need to influence, it becomes a fire."

"I see, so you're thinking of burning people alive." I was worried that might actually be the truth. Claudette's note reminded me to be vigilant and to remain guarded.

Edward shook his head with a slight laugh. His face relaxed as he closed his eyes, taking years off his age. He might only be a year or two older than me, but when he softened his features, he transformed into a young boy. I had no idea what he was doing, but seconds stretched as he focused on his thoughts.

And now the match is struck. The voice was gentle, a little distant, but loud enough I could make out his words. He did it with such ease, as if it really were a match, and with the flick of his wrist, he struck it against the side of the box. Could controlling the ghost be as simple as imagining a burning piece of wood?

"Now you try."

Closing my eyes and I imagined standing in a dark room. I knew I was in the space, but I couldn't see my imaginary hand as it waved in front of my face. What it would feel like if I held my hand out with a single match. I had done this a thousand times before at home, fumbling with a real matchbox, trying to light the oil lamp. It was almost as if I could roll the thin piece of wood between my fingers and feel the corners of the matchstick.

My muscles tensed as I pictured the match flickering to life. This was too simple. There was no way what Edward spoke of could work. I peeked to see him not quite frowning, somewhere closer to confused. There were no ghosts. No luck, perhaps because of how different our abilities were.

"I lit the match," I said, obviously annoyed.

"You didn't."

"Yes. I did."

"No. You did not," he said. "Try again."

I scoured at him, closing my eyes, expecting to see the same tiny dancing flame. To my surprise, he was correct. I imagined myself still holding a tiny, flameless piece of wood. There was no flame. I lit it again in my mind.

"It's—"

"No, it's not." Just like that, the match went out. I tried to recall what happened when he influenced the mobsters. There had been a weird echo with his voice. My lack of a tiny inferno was not because he influenced me. What game could he possibly be playing?

"How do you know?"

"Did you think it would be that easy? It's never that simple in the beginning. Now, light the match."

Frank liked to say I irritated easily. Susan Lee says the same. They were correct, I was getting aggravated. Edward's smug tone was about to get him a whopping. With almost no effort, I could stand and smack him across the face with the palm of my hand. Then we would see who could strike a match. Perhaps Frank was right, I'd look into my anger issues in the future.

I didn't imagine the flame coming to life so much as I imagined the air around the match catching on fire. I didn't want a tiny flame, something that might leave a small blister, no, I wanted a real fire. The ball of flame rested in my outstretched hand, burning brighter and brighter until it wrapped itself along my skin. The warmth radiating through my fingers was almost tangible, like it was happening in reality.

"Eleanor," Edward's voice cracked. He sat down on the bench, inches away from me.

When I opened my eyes, there were ghosts, hundreds upon hundreds of them. Phantom ducks swam in the pond while a lovely lady and her suitor also had ghosts. Even Edward's ghost pulled from his body, its hand resting gently on top of my phantom's hand.

"It worked," I said, shocked. The ghosts were singular, each living thing having only one. Their destinies were solidified, and I remained unable to alter the course. It wasn't quite what I longed for, but it served as a starting point.

Edward reached for my hand, but I beat him to the draw. I squeezed his fingers, giving a slight smile. I wanted to change the future, to intervene and challenge fate. It had been hopeless for so long, but for the first time, Edward restored my hope. Perhaps, if I was lucky, this was the beginning of something much bigger.

"That's enough training for today," he said. "Let's find ourselves lunch."

I didn't want to stop. Sitting in the park with Edward, I needed to push myself harder. I wanted to establish control over the ghosts. I wanted to master my abilities until they served me and not the other way around.

"There will be more on date two," he said, sensing my hesitation.

Date? I hadn't thought of it quite like that, but the idea wasn't a bad one.

"Food it is then." Yes, I would enjoy a second date with him.

Edward had plenty of charm. The thought continued to run amuck in my head as he rattled on about New York City. It was a gigantic place, and as he talked about the various boroughs, I realized I had seen very little of my home. But he spoke with excitement, and the zeal in his mannerisms reached an almost comical proportion.

"I stayed in Brooklyn for a while, it had friendly people. But that's not where the money is at. They're modest, small homes, families. Those are off-limits, I had nothing growing up, I wouldn't wish that on another kid."

He had morals, loose ones perhaps. His code of ethics involved only taking from people who had what he deemed "too much." I'm not sure I agreed, but at least he wasn't pond scum.

"Language barrier is a bit of a problem. Lots of Hebrew speakers, Germans, even Italians. They don't think in English."

"You can't understand their..." I paused, ensuring nobody was listening, "thoughts?"

Edward set down his knife and fork, a strange combination for slices of pizza. "Nope. I can sometimes make guesses, but it's just the same if I started speaking French to you. You follow the gist of it, but not the details."

He returned to cutting his slice of pizza and devouring it one bite at a time. On the other hand, I had nothing to prove to my date. I folded a slice in half and devoured a huge portion.

"I've been going on and on. What about you? How'd you get to New York?"

I considered my answer as I chomped away. I hid my face behind a napkin, speaking behind it despite half a slice of pizza filling my mouth. "Frank."

"You've mentioned him before. Who is this guy?"

The waitress stopped by our table with a metal pitcher of water. She reached for Edwards glass. "Leave us." I could hear the echo, the signal he influenced the woman. Without question, she retracted her hand and returned to her duties. His willingness to shove aside a person's freewill was a bit unnerving, but I hid my feelings while I finished swallowing my pizza.

"He was my dad's army buddy. When my parents died, he offered to take care of me. He was a Fire Fighter in New York. Frank's retired now because of his back. He runs a gym for vets. He's a stellar guy overall."

"Consider me jealous."

He didn't elaborate. The statement left me wondering if he was jealous of my father figure, or a man in my life worthy of such high praise.

"Frank's the second-best dad I could ask for." Really? I have no idea why I felt the need to soothe Edward's jealousy. But as he continued cutting his pizza, I couldn't help but feel a bit of warmth in my cheeks.

"You're not like other dames."

"I'll take that as a compliment."

He shook his head, trying to backpedal from the sideways statement. "I meant, they're always fixated on being dames. You're more like—"

"One of the men?"

He stopped chewing, realizing the next time he opened his mouth, he'd be inserting his foot.

"Don't worry, you're not the first to say it. My roommate, Susan Lee, is always commenting on my brutish ways. She gets worked up whenever I come home from training with Frank's army buddies. Apparently it's uncouth to have a black eye from boxing."

"You're *definitely* not like other dames."

The talk of the gym and fighting served as the perfect segue into the incident this morning. I had been trying to work out what I would tell Edward, but I didn't want to give away too much. Claudette's note remained tucked in my pocket and the thought of danger had me glancing down alleys as we ventured toward the restaurant.

"You're thinking of something serious. Did I say something wrong?"

I reached across the small table and rested my hand on his. He set down the fork and held my fingers. I tried to ignore the redness in my cheeks. It was important, more than important, it was a matter of life and death. After sitting with Edward in the park and having pizza at his favorite restaurant, I feared he might be on the killer's watch list.

"Have you heard about the serial killer in the city?"

"Not quite where I thought this was going," he admitted. "But yes, apparently it's the only thing New York cares about other than the war."

"I think I found a clue about the person behind the murders."

"Now you're a detective?"

I laughed as I brushed off the comment. Truth be told, I had considered it. If I could control the ghosts and make them work for me, I'd be an outstanding sleuth. Knowing the future is something the police could only dream of having. Perhaps someday, but I needed to focus, to stop the killer before I became a target. Or Claudette. Or Edward.

"I think he's hunting mentalists."

There was a range of emotion, his eyebrows contorting above his eye. He went from confusion to concern and even a bit of anger. I wondered if he thought about the implications, or just how he'd survive an encounter. It might very well be the first time somebody knew his secret and sought him out.

"I don't want you to get hurt," I said.

"I think I can handle myself." His ego spoke before he managed a reasonable reply.

"I believe he's immune to your influencing."

"He's a mentalist?" The waitress walked to our table and poured Edward a glass of water. He didn't speak, but I had to wonder if he had suggested she carry out her duties. He picked it up and took a gulp as she left, completely unaware of what was happening.

"I don't know."

"I can take care of myself," he said.

"Of course, but be careful, please." The *please* was to squash his ego and make it more of a plea. "I have a few leads I need to look into. If they pan out, you'll be the first to know."

He gave my hand a squeeze. "I'm not scared of some deranged killer, but thank you." He should be scared. Boys and their unearned bravado—he deserved to be slapped.

"Pardon me, but I have to go." I needed to head to the gym and speak with Frank. Working out would offer a chance to run through what I could have done differently at the herbal shop. I didn't want to leave Edward, but I wasn't ready for him to invade my life, at least not yet.

"Can I call you?" he asked.

"Can I reach out to you?" I tapped my forehead.

He nodded. "Just light the match and you'll be able to find me."

"I will." My cheeks turned a darker shade of red as I left. I wanted to invite him to the gym, to meet Frank, to watch me train. I had to stop myself as I thought of him in workout clothes, glistening in sweat. No, I was not ready for that, not yet.

Chapter Nineteen

"Why is nobody talking about it?"

My left fist grazed the bag before I leaned into my right hook. It jingled on the chain. Frank hovered to my side, watching my form, tapping my shoulder when I dropped my fists too low.

"You're stepping too close. Give yourself more room." He was right, of course. I wasn't giving myself enough space to throw my weight behind the punch. I repeated, it rattled even louder this time. "Good, now make sure you're not punching the bag, punch through the bag. Straighten out those wrists."

My wrists were straight, but he'd repeat the chant as long as I practiced. I had a tendency of dropping my guard, but I never bent my wrists. I couldn't afford another trip to the hospital. At this rate, I walked about town with bruises and scrapes. Eventually somebody would accuse Frank of manhandling me.

"How many dead now? Nine? I've lost track." I bobbed under an imaginary hook.

"There's a war overseas. People want to believe they're fighting for a peaceful country. It ruins the image when there is a murderer on the loose." He tapped me on the shoulder again. Either I was tired, or my mind drifted elsewhere. After nearly being cut open by a deranged serial killer, I thought a quick refresher would do me good.

Between Edward and the bomber jacket, my thoughts weren't in the here and now.

"There's no way people would rather be ignorant."

Again with the tapping on my shoulder. I was exhausted, my brain jumping from one topic to the next. I stepped back and instead of throwing a punch, I spun my leg from the side, the top of my foot hitting the bag hard enough to make it swing. Frank moved away, giving me room to maneuver.

Some men in the gym had shown me the basics of martial arts. I managed a handful of kicks and how to grapple a man and toss him over my shoulder. But I wanted to learn more, to become a fighter.

I braced myself as I leaned forward, kicking with the heel of my foot. The bag swung backward and as it came barreling back at me, I stepped to the side, spinning around. I drove my elbow into the bag. It lacked grace, but it wasn't like I had the opportunity to practice it on actual people. The men in the gym already feared I'd beat them in a match, adding kicks and spins would have them running from the ring.

"Okay, I think you've had enough today."

Frank grabbed the bag, stopping it from swinging. I panted while I wiped the sweat from my forehead. I might not be the best, but the next time I encountered the killer, I wouldn't be lying on my back like a helpless victim.

"Sorry," I said. "I have a lot on my mind."

"Me too," he held up his arm, pointing at the bandage. "If it wasn't for Claudette, both of us might be six feet under."

The sigh was less from exhaustion, and more an action to push doubts out of my head. The visualizations helped center myself. How it eluded me to use the technique for *other* parts of my life left me baffled. I closed my eyes as I pulled the tape from my hand. The match, I struck it, and I could feel the warmth of the light as it blazed.

"You okay, 'Nore?"

"Shhh." With a flip of my imaginary wrist, the match vanished and the tiny flame rested in my hand. Edward would say it wasn't lit, I'd argue. Something between the visualization and the anger summoned the ghosts. The image of a flame wasn't enough. It needed fuel, emotional tinder. My first thought was the man in the bomber jacket hovering over me. I had been a victim, unable to defend myself. Fear.

The fire grew.

"I see them, Frank."

Sitting in a circle between the free weights and the boxing ring, a meeting of eight men sat listening intently. A specter of Frank's future-self spoke to the group, speaking passionately, hand gestures reinforcing his words. I'm sure if I pushed, I could transform his mumbles into coherent sounds. I recognized several of them. Vincent and Michael sat opposite one another.

The real Frank stood at my side, following my line of sight, confused at the statement. I withdrew, not wanting to invade his privacy. The ghosts faded.

"The ghosts?"

"You were speaking at your group." I reached for his hand, squeezing it tightly. "Tonight, I'm sure it was tonight. I can't hear them, but they came when I asked." My voice was shaky. I felt overwhelmed at the prospect of being in control. I didn't fight it as my eyes glossed over with tears.

There were more, hundreds even. Men lifted weights, trained in the ring, while dozens of phantom Franks assisted in their workouts. There were the regulars I recognized, but it seemed as if Frank opened his doors to a fresh wave of patrons. They all had a similar look, short-cropped hair and thin, rugged types.

"The war is over," I said with a smile. "They're young, Frank. It's not just the wounded finding their way. You're guiding them all."

Frank's fingers tightened about my hand. He was many things to the world, but being a protector of wayward souls had become a large part of his identity. I was proud of the man, my heart swelling with love for the big lug.

"Michael," I gasped. His ghost pushed at the wheels of his chair, gliding toward where we stood now. Unlike the others, this one was nearly opaque. I had to wonder if that indicated how close it was to happening. Without indicators like a newspaper or a clock, it was impossible for me to sort the timeline.

He spoke to a phantom of Frank. The words turned clear, audible, and almost as loud as if he were in the room with me.

"I need help," he said.

"Frank," I said, "it's Michael. Something is wrong."

The ghosts evaporated, and the image of the flame turned dark as I caught the real Michael in the doorway leading to the gym. I let go of Frank's hand, realizing the future was about to come true.

"He needs your support," I whispered.

I finished pulling at the tape around my other hand as Michael approached. I waved. "Nice seeing you again."

He gave a slight bow in the chair. "You brighten my day, Eleanor." I blushed at the compliment. It was rare to meet a proper gentleman.

I stepped away, clinging to the lengthy pieces of tape. "I'm going to hit the showers. Michael, it's always a pleasure to see a man as dashing as you. At some point, you will need to escort me for coffee."

It was his turn to blush. I gave him a pat on the shoulder as I walked toward the locker room. I could hear Michael speak softly as I left. "Frank, can I talk to you?"

Not a victim.

The words continued to roll around in my brain as I threw my clothes in my locker. Staring at the bandage on my arm, I replayed the scene. Could I have stepped back, or thrown an elbow to change the outcome? The ghosts had given me an advantage in the ring, but this thing, he pushed through my foresight with sheer brutality.

He charged with his weapon drawn. I focused on the blade, ignoring the man wielding it. That had been my mistake, I missed the obvious opening. Pushing his arm out wide, I could have driven the heel of my palm into his sternum or forced knuckles into his throat. I'm not sure even the most skilled fighter could have determined the killer's persistence. I shouldn't have gone from savior to victim in a few short seconds.

With my eyes closed, the outcome changed—the man's chest

burst. Claudette ended the fight, and I swore my chest ached as the bullet sailed freely from the man into my own. My eyes flew open as I gasped out loud.

"If I had fought him, would I have died?" I didn't know the answer. Claudette's shot may have penetrated him and killed me in the process. The hair along my arms stood on high alert. I spun about, expecting Frank or Michael to be standing in the doorway.

"Hello?" Nobody returned the greeting. The paranoia settled in. Frank wouldn't allow any of the men to enter the locker room with me inside. I refused to let fear guide me, then I realized, the bullet wouldn't have killed me.

"I'm invincible," I whispered, recalling an elder me dying on a plush rug.

Very few people would find visions of their death as comforting as me. I knew how I died. I might not know when, but it was decades in my future and I knew where. Today, even if the bullet had struck me, I would have survived. I would have been hurt, perhaps crippled, but death would not come knocking for me.

It wasn't as much a comfort as it was a freeing sensation. I could have fought back or have been the victim. I could have done *anything* this morning. Frank, though, I had never seen his demise, so he was at risk, and Claudette's death might still become a reality, but I stood outside the grasp of Heaven and Hell. No, not freeing, empowering.

"I'm coming for you," I whispered.

The ghosts snapped into existence, dozens of them filling the locker room as if they had taken up permanent residence in the after-life. If men had been with me, the laughter creeping from my belly would have been less than welcome. Emotionally charged with a renewed zeal to stop the nasty thing in the bomber jacket, the ghosts took advantage. The copious amounts of naked flesh might have made me blush, but I was Eleanor Bouvier. I *was* invulnerable.

In the shower I spun the nozzle, waiting patiently as the water reached a satisfying piping hot. I stepped through a ghost of Vincent showering to let it pelt against my chest. Before I could reach the soap, the hair on my arms pointed skyward.

"I know you're there," I whispered.

A flicker, a flame, a hand consumed by orange and red. I didn't need the ghosts of injured servicemen, I needed my own. Through phantom eyes, I watched as the room spun about. My ghost emerged, looking into the sea of bodies. Unlike the other transparencies, one maintained a shimmer of color.

I know you're there.

How? Edward's voice reverberated somewhere in my head. I couldn't hear the words so much as know what he said.

I lit the match.

So you did. It impressed him. He stepped forward while I struggled to maintain my focus. The water beating against my chest felt like a memory from days past.

Edward wasn't a ghost, not like the ones I was used to seeing. Whatever approached, it wasn't a vision. As he stared at me, maintaining eye contact, I got the distinct impression my ghost was the only one he could see.

How are you doing this? I asked.

Remote viewing. Some of us are better at it than others. I can't do it with a human, but with another mentalist to guide me, I can find them.

I brought you here?

He smiled, that charming, devilish grin I couldn't help but return. For the first time, his eyes dipped low, admiring more than my talents. I wouldn't have known how to protest even if I wanted. The shift from a grinning boy turned serious as he contemplated something more carnal.

Like what you see?

The transparent image of him closed the space between us as he bit his lower lip. I was intrigued, to say the least. Adored in the shower of a locker room by an invisible mentalist brought with it a slew of interesting possibilities. He wore the same clothes from earlier, but I suddenly had the desire to see the man underneath.

The more I saw, the more I desired. Edward's voice held a sensation of yearning. He reached for my face, resting his hand on my cheek. I turned around and stepped into the place where my ghost had been. I could only see him with my specter, but I knew he was still in the room.

Come with me.

I covered my cheek with my hand, imagining his thumb

caressing my damp skin. He was indeed handsome. I even entertained the idea of saying yes to another encounter, but I didn't imagine he'd see me naked after our first date. But now that he had, my body craved more than the memory of his touch.

I forgot the water and the chilled air as Edward pulled me into the white room. Unlike before, there was no infinite space or blinding light. It became an oxymoron, it was now filled with black and a single lamp atop a nightstand illuminated a bed with decadent maroon sheets.

Edward snaked between the sheets, his bare chest standing out against the wine-colored fabric. He pulled back the sheet to his side, patting it gently. I had no idea how my body reacted in the real world as I climbed in next to the dashing man.

He held me close, his lips pressing against mine. His tongue penetrated my lips while his body ground against my own. What little reserve I had faded. I grabbed him by the wrists and pinned him to the bed.

"I'm here," I whispered.

Chapter Twenty

Each kiss held an urgency, a need to steal my breath as if he might die of suffocation. The stubble, the tender bites, the taste, each was as intense as if he stood in the locker room. I leaned back, still pinning his wrists to the bed, and I gasped as the sensation of water pelting my shoulders and running down my body.

"We occupy two worlds, the here and there." Even his voice sounded only feet away.

The now and then.

"They'll worry if I take too long," I said.

He sat upright, wrapping his arm around my waist. He brushed the hair from my cheek, letting his fingers caress the line of my jaw. "Here, time can flow as quickly or slowly as we will it." He kissed along my neck, lingering over my clavicle. Dragging his lips down my chest, his breath warmed my skin. Each time he kissed my body, a current ran down my spine.

Edward spoke the most seductive words. "Here, time has no meaning."

His lips hovered over my nipple, and if I arched my back, it'd begin a cascade. His eyes rolled up, confident and willing, but hesitant. Every time he exhaled, I had to withhold a gasp. He made no move, no ravishing, just a fire in his eyes.

I had experienced my share of trysts with handsome men. Some names I knew, others I long forgot. But Edward was unlike the ones I'd discarded. It wasn't the walk in the park or the dinner that gave him real estate in my mind. Edward approached virgin territory. I had squandered my innocence as a young woman, but here we were, two mentalists on the verge of an act more intimate than any sex.

"Are you sure?" The words were breathy. Each syllable beat against my skin and the knot in my stomach loosened. I bowed my spine, my breast connecting with his lips. His hands on my back tightened. First, he ran his tongue along my nipple, tugging at it with his teeth. I whimpered my approval.

My fingers slid through Edward's hair, the sensation as electric as if we occupied the same bed. When I grabbed him by the back of the head and pulled him against my breast, he took the cue. He bit down, finding the thin line between pleasure and pain.

He shifted his weight, rolling us about until I laid on my back with him above me. I expected that boyish grin to appear and expose his teeth, but his eyes scoured my body, working from my navel to my face, and there was nothing youthful or innocent about him. Unlike those before him, he took his time, savoring the experience.

You're beautiful.

His whispers were laced with a sense of awe. The words penetrated my mind and coiled around my spine until it reached my stomach. With each encounter before, I used the men as an escape. I never worried if they found me attractive because there were no emotions exchanged. But in the white room, Edward's affection couldn't be clearer if he wrote them down.

I was no longer alone.

Pushing myself up, I kissed him. "I want you."

Edward needed nothing more. He slid down the bed, kissing along my belly and down my inner thigh. I reached behind me, fingers digging into a pillow. He worked his way to my other leg. I moaned my approval, trying desperately to not grab him by the back of the head.

And then it happened. The tip of his tongue made contact and my back arched. I suspected with such a devilish grin, it wouldn't have been his first time. Now I knew. He expertly explored my body. I never wanted him to stop.

For a split second, I worried I might fall in the shower. When I opened my eyes, I stood in the locker room. I was about to call out for Edward when he stepped behind me. I spun about, admiring the way his abs created an arrow pointing toward his manhood. He stood at attention, ready to continue our love making.

"Are we really here?" I asked.

"Is it important?"

"No." The word could barely be heard over the water splashing against our bodies. I could be standing in the same spot as my physical body, but I didn't know or care. The change of scenery only made it more enticing. Edward's willingness here in the shower left me wanting him more.

He stepped up behind me, nudging me forward until my hands braced against the wall. With one hand, he held my hips firmly, and with a control I never granted other men. His cock slid between my legs. With a slight wiggle, he found the mark, and I gasped.

His strokes varied between short and quick and long and slow. I reached for my hip, placing my hand over his. He spread his fingers, and they linked together. He reached around with his other hand, resting it on my sternum, inches from my heart. His thrusting grew sporadic, and I moaned, enthralled by his vigor.

His movement turned erratic, and I knew he was close. The sensation, a thousand tiny zaps of electricity, surged through my body each time his hands touched my skin. I found it difficult to breathe, and I wanted to scream in ecstasy.

He grunted but refused to quit. The growl became a low moan but couldn't compare to my own. I cried out as I shivered. The warmth spread throughout my body and left me trembling.

Edward's fingers tapped against my chest, rapidly at first, now slowing. I nearly commented on the odd behavior. The finger matched the rhythm of my heart. I leaned back as he mirrored the beating in my chest. He kissed my neck as his body pressed against my skin. I swore I could feel his heart synchronize in harmony with my own.

It wasn't enough that our bodies locked together. His admiration whispered about me as if he shared the words out loud. "You need to go."

"No," I sighed, "I don't want this to end."

"This isn't a one-time encounter," he assured. I didn't need to see the future to know he spoke the truth.

The water pelted along my torso. I was left in the locker room, without Edward pressed into the curve of my back. Touching my chest, my body recalled every sensation. My legs threatened to buckle as I stood in the spray. Despite the event taking place in our minds, my body acknowledged it as being reality.

I blushed from the brazen affair, partly because it happened, but mostly because I wanted more.

Soon, very soon.

Chapter Twenty-One

I stood over the stove as I waited for the kettle to whistle. Between the bomber jacket man, a thorough workout at the gym, and a... I didn't need a mirror to know I was blushing. Just the thought of Edward without clothes made my stomach flutter. I had never seen him naked, nor let him touch my skin, but my body knew him intimately.

I stayed at the gym long enough the previous night to help Frank take out the trash and arrange the chairs in their familiar circle. I couldn't help but think of Michael. There was a bit of sadness that he had fallen prey to the siren's call of alcohol, but I was grateful he took the first step toward recovery.

Frank demanded I be careful when I left my apartment today. He didn't beg me to stay indoors like a shut-in, but he made sure I acknowledged the risk every time I stepped outside my door. I appreciated his fatherly instincts and his constant respect for my boundaries. There was no doubt in his mind, I'd be prowling the streets, searching for the man in the bomber jacket.

"There's not going to be any water left," Susan Lee said, breaking my reverie.

The whistling had grown loud enough, I must have ignored it for at least a minute. I flipped off the burner and pulled the kettle to the side. I needed coffee, a kick in the pants to help me plow through the changes that occurred over the past few days.

"Are you doing okay?" Susan Lee's voice held her signature worry. Most of the time it was because of my watching the ghosts and ignoring her. I caught her eyes fixated on my bandaged arm.

"I cut myself on a bottle taking out the trash. It stung something nasty." The lies were almost too easy at this point.

"Let me grab a bandage and I'll wrap it for you. Frank isn't exactly a field medic." I didn't object, it'd fall on deaf ears. Instead, I poured a cup of scalding water for myself and Susan Lee. I added the instant coffee, stirring vigorously and adding a half spoon of sugar to her cup.

It wasn't a particularly pleasant taste, but it did the trick. The bitter coffee served as a precursor to heading onto the streets. Claudette would be on my rounds today. Without Frank nearby, I'd be able to ask her to elaborate on the note.

"Give me your arm, we'll have you right as rain." She peeled off the bandage, and I braced myself for a gash worthy of stitches. Susan Lee frowned, unamused at my hissing. "For a woman who beats up men, you're certainly a wimp."

There should have been a clean cut almost four inches long on my forearm. The depth of the bomber's blade was enough that it had hardly registered at the time. Now, to look at the scar, I would think an overzealous kitten on a catnip binge had scratched me. I hadn't put stock into Claudette's concoction, but now, I would ask her if she had something to ease the bruising on my ribs.

"A bruise doesn't have blood," I tried to rebound.

"Neither does this, you scaredy cat." She dabbed a cotton ball covered in alcohol on the cut. With a few Band-Aids, she hid the scrape. I wondered if there'd be a scar or if Claudette's elixir would leave my skin as clean as before.

Strategic topic change. "I talked to Frank and the men at the gym and they reluctantly agreed. Frank is requiring them to volunteer an hour each day before they show up to work out."

"The socks?" Susan Lee had an agenda that wouldn't relent. They might find her enthusiasm a bit too much, but I had to admit, she served as a positive influence.

"I left before the meeting, but he promised he would ask. Don't hold your breath. Those men are a little rougher around the edges than his typical gym buddies."

"Oh, Eleanor, thank you so much."

I would regret the next statement. "Susan Lee, I don't say this nearly enough, but you're an inspiration. I'm not sure how you conjure such optimism, but each morning I leave thinking about how I can change the world."

The cup of coffee in her hand shook, spilling a bit of the liquid. She sat down at the kitchen table, clasping her hands together. Let it be known, this is why I try to avoid being emotional. Somewhere buried in my ribcage, there is a heart, and each time it reveals itself, somebody cries.

"Eleanor," she sniffled, drying her eyes with the back of her hand.

"If I knew it was going to make you cry—"

"Don't ruin a perfectly sweet moment," she swatted at my shoulder. She gave a slight chuckle. "And here I thought you're the brave one. You take gruff from nobody. I don't know how you do it. I wish I could be more like you."

She dragged me into her emotional mess. The tears started, first my left eye, then my right. I couldn't resist after a compliment of that magnitude. "Oh, look what you've done, Susan Lee."

We both laughed as I leaned over and gave her a hug. This emotional start to my day was becoming a bit too common. Yesterday I entertained her turning a gym into a volunteer center and then faced a killer. Now I was crying in the kitchen. By lunch I might single-handedly win the war.

"How about this," Susan Lee started, "I'll keep you compassionate and you keep reminding me to be strong."

"I can agree to that." Susan Lee's intuition had partly uncovered the reason I continued rooming with her. Every now and then, I needed prodding for the walls to come crumbling down. Once I put myself back together, it'd be time to begin the prowl for the killer.

"I like to believe a woman with a little support from her sisters can take on the world."

True, Susan Lee, very true.

Every time I passed an alley, I made sure to step into the street. I'd ease my way by, checking to see if an ominous crazy man waited to pull me into the shadows. I might be invincible, but I preferred having the upper hand when I found the killer. Knowing he was tracking mentalists meant checking in with Claudette and Edward frequently.

Edward had shown me how to summon the ghosts and, more importantly, how to calm their angry determination. It was a bit odd to think about living in the moment. For the first time since I was a young girl, I saw the world as it was, not as it would someday be.

Claudette, however, had brought visions to the surface. They were opposite sides of the same coin. Both allowed me to witness things that hadn't happened, but the ghosts gave me a glimpse into the immediate future. The visions, if I could harness them, would allow me to see the bigger picture, a world days or perhaps years away. Between the two, I'd be a master of the yet to come.

I had a destination in mind before seeing Claudette. The discussion with Susan Lee had brought something to the surface, a determination. I wasn't looking for a killer to save myself, or even to protect other mentalists, it was because I was the only one capable of correcting this. Edward couldn't influence the killer, and Claudette was a healer. These were the ideas Frank often referred to as my dangerous aspirations.

He was right, I needed to make sure I protected myself. I stepped inside the used clothing store. There were practical clothes near the front, shirts and trousers lining the walls, a complete smorgasbord of cost-saving garments. I wasn't here to save money, at least not for a shirt.

"Can I help you, ma'am?"

The gentleman in the shop must have been pushing sixty, too old for the war effort. He wore a snappy suit, appearing quite the dashing silver fox. The thickness of his glasses made his green eyes shine. The moment he spotted my lack of skirt and flowing blouse, he gave a slight smile.

"You look like a woman on the hunt for adventure."

He wasn't wrong. "You could say that."

The man leaned over the counter, just past the till. He looked me up and down. I could tell he attempted to pinpoint what type of woman I might be. I decided to let him speculate.

"A solo adventurer, a traveler perhaps?"

"Not quite, or at least not yet."

"Hmm," he pulled off his glasses and gave them a slight polish before putting them back on. I thumbed through the shirts on the rack. Most were more delicate than I typically wore. However, I came across more than one garment that reminded me of Susan Lee.

"You're a fighter," he said with a bit of disbelief.

"How—"

"I spent my younger years in the ring. I recognize the stance. No, you're not looking for travel. You're seeking a fight."

"Correct."

"Be careful, lassie, terrible things on the streets these days." Where many men might try to convince me otherwise, he simply offered a word of caution. The world needed more people like him.

"I'm interested in that motorcycle jacket in the window."

He leaned over the counter, past the cash register to see it hanging in the front of the store. The clerk leaned back, shaking his head. "I'm sorry, but I can't sell you that, it's a man's motorcycle jacket."

I reached into my pocket, fishing out my wallet, prepared to slap money on the table and take it. This morning I shared a sweet and tender moment with Susan Lee, talking about lifting women up. I had labeled the man incorrectly. Men like him are the ones who tried to keep us contained.

"I have a couple jackets back here much more suited for you," I flipped open my wallet, staring at the green paper notes. He shuffled through a rack behind the counter and pulled out a woman's double-breasted leather jacket. "I suspect it might even fit you."

At the rate I received positivity, I feared the other shoe would drop at any moment. "That is lovely," I said.

"Don't be offended at my presumptions, but you strike me as an adventurer. But by the way your trousers fit, it looks like you are set on adventuring as only a woman can."

"The very best kind, I'd say." There was hope, the seeds of progress being sewn. I had to remember, hidden away, a silent army grew, and soon we'd stampede the world bringing about change.

"My late wife would agree. She'd say men lack the cunning to go on real adventures. I was lucky she let me tag along for the ride."

"Your wife sounds like a woman I would have admired."

He handed me the jacket. It had been well worn, the joints soft and tender. The clerk stepped behind me, helping me into it. Chivalry wasn't dead, just hard to find.

He helped button the jacket, oblivious to my breasts as he tucked the collar back. I rotated my shoulders and I was surprised at the free range of motion. With a quick buckle of the belt, I not only felt ready for an adventure, I looked the part.

"It's amazing," I stepped in front of a mirror and caught a glimpse of myself. The jacket was rugged but feminine. It hugged my body in the right spots and I had to say, I did indeed feel as if I could take on the world.

"How much?" I asked, reaching for my wallet again.

"Judith would be angry if I charged you for her jacket. She'd be happy to know it was going back out into the world."

"Are you sure? I don't want to take away a memory of her."

"Oh dear, no. You're not taking away a memory, just a jacket. The memories stay with me. Go make your own."

"Once I've had my adventure, I'll come back and we can swap tales."

"Judith would have liked that."

The dust from the shop tickled my nose until I sneezed. I exchanged a pleasant handshake and exited onto the street. I didn't need another piece of clothing, but something about my conversation with Susan Lee left me yearning for a change. Good things were about to happen.

"Good things *can* happen." I reaffirmed, not quite believing it, not yet. Hope managed to seep its way into my heart. There were many deeds necessary before I turned into an optimist, but it was a start. With an emerging outlook, I needed a change for my exterior.

I slid my hands in the pockets, getting used to the feeling. My hand brushed something stiff. I pulled out a small square, a photograph of a middle-aged woman and the store clerk. I smiled at the way she boldly stared at the camera and he had his arm wrapped around her waist. The photo told of a romance extending beyond death.

In the photograph he too wore a similar jacket, and I looked up to see the mannequin in the window. I assumed he had volunteered this jacket because it would fit more appropriately, but I had to wonder. Perhaps he still had another adventure or two left in him.

I had one more stop before visiting Claudette. Before I kicked off this journey, I needed to check in on an acquaintance and call upon her services. I tucked the keepsake gently inside the breast pocket, a reminder of why I wore it. As I walked, I no longer dodged the alleys.

"Bomber jacket, you should be the one who's scared."

It was mid-afternoon before I reached Claudette's shop. My errands had run longer than expected, but I was feeling excited. Emma Jean had been pleasantly surprised to see me and even more thrilled when I asked her to make adjustments to my jacket. She didn't ask questions or raise an eyebrow at my odd requests, she simply agreed and took the garment. Even her boss was mildly pleasant, I'm sure because she knew a profit when she saw one.

"Eleanor, I did not expect to see you so soon. I assumed it would require a killer to bring you to my shop again."

I couldn't entirely tell if she was joking or if she suspected I used her as a means to an end. Eventually, I would get to the conversation of the killer, but for now, I wanted to know more about her, the angels, and the Lao. But I found it difficult to surprise the woman.

"Something has changed, child. The angels, they're not vibrating like they were. You're different." Claudette might be able to sense the otherworldliness of the ghosts, but even she had limitations. I wondered if she still had her gifts if she'd be capable of divining specifics.

"I uhm..." I trailed off. There was no point in trying to describe things I couldn't explain. I turned to slowly shut the door, closing my eyes at the same time. There in my mind, I imagined my hand stretched out before me. The first attempt didn't ignite the fire. I tried again to no avail.

"What's wrong, child?"

This morning I confessed to my roommate an affection born of sisterhood. We laughed and cried as we finally found our common ground. Susan Lee's laughter was like wind chimes caught in a tornado, beautiful, and chaotic. The tiny flame in my mind sprung from my palm.

"Child…"

I fed the fire, my desire to be better, to be more. There were insecurities, uncertainties, and even a hesitation from my past. I shoved those feelings into it, imagining them as kindling only served to fuel the flame. I locked away my emotions for so long, it was refreshing to own them, even if they were terrifying.

The tiny flicker roared, spitting bits around my hand. The center of the flame bled from red to orange to yellow, a beautiful cascade of emotional fire. I turned to see the shop filled with hundreds of ghosts. Most of them Claudette, but now and then a patron stepped through me, speaking with her before she went on a quest to fulfill their needs from the jars.

"The Lao," she whispered.

"I have to talk to you," I said as I closed my hand. The fire didn't vanish at first. I had to push a bit at the image, shaking my imaginary hand. I finally calmed the flame and the ghosts in the room faded.

"It seems you do, child." She pulled a stool from behind the counter and set it next to hers. She perched herself atop it, leaning on the table, her expression eager for details.

"But first, tell me about the man."

"The killer?"

"No, child, your lover."

Chapter Twenty-Two

"… and here I am."

I spent the better part of an hour confessing about Edward —*Everything*. Claudette nodded her head, listening to every word. I tried to glaze over the more intimate notes, but she gave me a look telling me she knew each time I attempted to skimp on the details.

As I finished, she leaned back on the stool and stretched her arms. She was a slender woman, but as she flexed, I discovered she was far more muscular than she let on. She let out a low whistle.

"Child, that is quite a productive week."

"I guess so." I always assumed change happened a bit at a time, so gradually, we hardly noticed until we reflected. Seeing the future allowed me to miss smaller moments. Now, after everything that took place, it felt like change simply broke through one wall after another, leaving a trail of crushed bricks in its wake.

"I get no feelings for this Edward," she said, waving her hand through the air. She spun about, feeling for some invisible force. "He remains a mystery to me."

"Is that bad?"

"It is neither good nor bad. It can mean many things, or nothing at all." Her rhetoric was almost as uncanny as her intuition. "Sorry, it's not the help you seek."

"Life must have a bit of mystery, I guess."

Claudette stood from her perch, giving a slight groan as she straightened her back. Her steps were hobbled as she eased the ache from her knees. Despite the signs of age, I couldn't place how old she might be. She hovered somewhere between a healthy sixty-five or a worn forty-year-old.

"What of the visions?" she asked.

"I tried the tea, it worked. Almost too well. It's going to sound crazy, but I saw a green woman with wings. She looked as if she might be meditating. Then she jumped through my bedroom wall and flew away."

"Perhaps a symbol of a future yet to pass?"

I shook my head. "I never see the symbolism. The visions are always things that will someday happen. At some time, there will be a green woman with wings. I just..." It sounded crazy, more so than usual. "With no context, I don't understand. Perhaps she's an alien? Like on the radio?"

"Perhaps," Claudette said. "There's no need to speculate on the ones that make no sense. In time, the Lao will reveal the rest."

"The second was the thing in the bomber jacket killing a man. He was like us, I'm certain of it. He attempted to do the same trick Edward does. He looked surprised when it didn't work. Is it possible he's immune to a mentalist's influence?"

"It would not surprise me. There is always a balance, if somebody sees forward, somebody, too, must see back."

I bit my tongue as my thoughts turned to Susan Lee. I had never met a person without a ghost, one who appeared on command, or of its own choosing. Try as I might, I couldn't see her future. I had to wonder if she was the counterbalance to my visions?

"The killer was ruthless, almost animalistic. He hardly staggered when struck, and it seemed as if he only had one purpose."

"I believe that is true," Claudette said. "My people speak of such monstrosities. With the right mixture, it is possible to rob a man of his will and turn him into a zombi. He has only the purpose of his creator, a single driving force."

"You think the killer is one of those?"

"Perhaps," she said. "The toxin makes the body slow, not like your killer. They are similar in their drive, but not in how they are made."

"You believe he was made?" The idea that the killer was only the henchman of a more dangerous person sent a shiver down my spine. More so, what did they hope to achieve by killing the mentalists in New York?

"Why would somebody allow himself to be a slave? Unless…" she paused, "we are only seeing one face of the devil? Perhaps something made him this way."

"Why is it after mentalists? There has to be a reason."

Claudette shook her head. "The first thing you must learn about evil, it has no reason. It simply is. A man may have his reasons, greed, jealousy, power, but ultimately, he does evil things because he is evil. That is his true purpose."

I'm not sure I agreed with her cut and dry assessment. If mentalists were being wiped out of existence, somebody wanted them gone. They might be evil, but being methodical meant motive. Once I discovered that, I would be one step closer to not only finding the killer, but also discovering the killer's boss. Without realizing it, the plot had thickened.

"Do they hate us?"

"Have you told others about your gifts?"

I shook my head. "No, I—"

"Because you're worried about how they might react. It is in man's nature to fear what they don't understand. To say you can see the future would open the flood gates and you'd never be free of their questions, or worst, their punishments."

"I don't—"

Claudette cut me off. "Witches were burned, after all." She pursed her lips and cocked her head, her hands firmly planted on her hips. The woman was waiting for me to question her statement. I couldn't argue. She was right. If word got out that I could see the future, the entire fate of mankind could change. But would that be a horrible thing?

"What of your last vision?"

I spilled the gruesome reality quickly. "I saw a chalk outline the police make. It was over there." I pointed to a spot on her floor. "It was close to your shape. I believe it was a vision of hours after your murder."

"My murder? Are you sure you are not misinterpreting?"

I nodded. The news didn't disturb her as much as I expected. Even at her age, I imagined disbelief and refusal to accept death, while so many things were left unaccomplished. Claudette didn't appear thrilled with the idea, but she didn't beg for more time either.

"Do you know when?"

I shook my head. "I couldn't find anything in the room with a date on it. It was early morning by the light. My best bet is that it happens at night."

Claudette thought about it for a moment and then waved off the statement. "There is no point in worrying about a future that has yet to happen. The most I can do is confront my fate with grace and dignity, child."

"Wow." I hadn't expected her to be so willing to fade into the ether.

"Meet grace," she held up her fist, "and dignity," the other joined. She clenched her hands tightly, the muscle in her upper body flexing. "Claudette will not go down without a fight."

I pulled out the slip of paper from my pocket, unsure how to bring up a conversation that could put her at odds with Frank. I set it down on the table, flattening out the wrinkles.

"What did you mean, danger?"

"I sense it about you, more than that, somebody close to you is in danger." She returned to the stool, gathering candles on the table. She struck a match, igniting each of the wicks, and gestured for me to sit opposite of her. I nervously joined, unsure of what she was doing.

"You visualize fire," she said calmly. Claudette's ability to know the unknown was uncanny, and yet she was unaware that her own death fast approached.

"I might not see the angels like you, but if they need to speak to me, they find a way. I am their humble servant." I didn't understand, not at that moment. Did she have abilities like me or not? Were there more flavors of these gifts than I realized? If so, what exactly could Claudette do?

"There is a man," she mumbled. Her eyes shut as she raised her hands up on the table. Her muscles relaxed as she drifted off elsewhere. She flinched. "A guide. He is in danger. The angels, they have nothing more to tell me. Whatever journey is before you, you must travel on your own." The candles flickered for a moment, enough that I thought they may blow out. Did Claudette really hear voices? Were angels real?

I feared for Edward. With that thing hunting mentalists, the only two mentors I had were in danger. If I didn't stop it soon, I would be alone again. That couldn't happen.

"I'm going to stop the killer," I said, determined. I banged my fist on the table hard enough that the candles jumped. Claudette caught one before it could fall. No matter what it took, this would end.

"I have no doubt, child," Claudette said, "I have no doubt."

Chapter Twenty-Three

The fence hadn't been repaired since Poppa left for the army. I could remember a long time ago that we had four cows, one for each of us. Mine had a black face with two white circles around her eyes. I named her Dorothy. Momma had shown us how to milk them, and each day it was my duty while Benjie helped. He was too young to lift the bucket, so instead he watched, asking over and over how much longer it would take.

The hammer made a ticking noise as Poppa held the nail between two fingers, gently tapping it. My job was to hold the board in place while he nailed it back to the post. We had nearly finished repairing the fence. Next would come finding new cows.

"Can I get a brown one?" I asked.

"A brown cow? We can see about that. You know they don't make chocolate milk."

I giggled. Of course I knew that. "I'm going to name her Toto."

"Toto the cow?" He chuckled. "I guess that's as good a name as any other."

He pulled away his fingers and the nail almost hovered in place as he drew the hammer back. Three smacks and it was all the way in. Now we only had two more to go.

"I bet Momma and Benjie aren't as close to being done as we are."

They had been assigned the task of cleaning out the hen house to prepare for a new set of birds. I disliked the chickens, they weren't as cute or cuddly as the cows. Benjie was old enough now that he could collect the eggs on his own. I'd get the milk, and he could risk being pecked. I wasn't excited for a rooster again, either. They were incredibly loud and often woke me hours before I needed to go to school.

"Two more and the fence is good to go. Then we can look at repairing the barn doors."

I forgot how much Poppa made us work when he was home. Before he left, we sold the cows and slaughtered the chickens. The fields were tended by the neighbors, and occasionally one of them would come over and help fix things around the house. But with Poppa home, he wanted Benjie and I to be able to run the farm.

"Are you going to plant wheat again?"

"Not this season, but maybe next year." Instead of crops, he had started working on the small garden behind the house. He liked to remind us that the food on the table was there because of our hard work. I hated getting dirty, but I loved spending time with him.

"I don't know if I want to be a farmer when I grow up," I admitted.

"Oh? What do you want to do?"

I hadn't thought about it. I didn't want to be covered in dirt all the time. Perhaps I could work at the hospital in one of the bigger towns. Or better yet, I could be like Dorothy and explore the world. Oh, I knew!

"I want to write books like *The Wonderful Wizard of Oz*."

"A writer, huh? I can see you doing that."

He lifted a piece of the fence that had come loose and fallen into the grass. Wedging it into place, he nodded toward the board and as his favorite helper, I rushed in. Holding the plank, he pulled nails out of his overalls and banged them into the post. The wood vibrated with each strike and my hands tingled, making me giggle.

"What are you going to write about?"

"Not about living on a farm." I shook my head to reinforce the point. "I want to write about far-away lands. Maybe about princesses who slay dragons."

He chuckled. "A princess? Nah, not a princess."

I nearly dropped the board at his disbelief. He stepped around me and started hammering in the other side of the plank. "Princesses are scared dames hiding in a castle. You should write about a young girl, a warrior. She can fight the evil dragons."

"Not evil, Poppa," I cried. "He's her pet. She rides him."

"That certainly sounds like a warrior to me!"

He finished pounding the nail and gave the board a good shake to ensure it wouldn't fall. He walked by my side as we headed to the final broken post. I could see him scanning the fields, the look on his face all squished, like he was thinking really hard. I followed his eyes and saw the dark clouds swirling about in the distance. They were beautiful, the way they chased each other in the sky. I knew from school they could become a tornado. If I had been by myself, I'd have run home.

"Tornado?" I asked.

"Perhaps," he said, lifting the last board up from the grass. "Either way, it looks like a storm is coming."

"How can you tell?" I squinted, looking for rain.

"You can taste it in the air. If you hold up your arm, you can see the little hairs starting to stand up. It means there's lightning coming."

I inspected the little clear hairs on my arm. I was about to call him a liar when I found several standing on end. Holding it up, I pointed. "There's lightning! Shouldn't we run back to the house? Momma always says when we see a storm, we should run home as fast as we can."

"You shouldn't be scared of the storm," he said, nodding to the board he held against the fence posts. I held it up while he got to work hammering. He repeated the same procedure, while I looked over my shoulder, wondering how long it would take me to run to the house.

"Poppa, who's that on our porch?"

He glanced up for a moment and then returned to hammering nails. The man on the porch was standing there, his arms hidden

149

behind his back. I couldn't make out his face, but he looked like Poppa when he got home from saving the world. He didn't budge, but his green tan uniform stood out against the white side of the house.

"Storms can be scary, Ellie, but you're not a little girl anymore. You can survive any storm. I'm sure of it."

The wind picked up, and the grass clapped at the hard gusts. I tried to hide being scared. Like in *The Wonderful Wizard of Oz*, we were told at school to fear of dark clouds. The wind could spin around and around until it made a funnel that would snatch us up if we didn't hide under our desks. I knew Poppa wouldn't let that happen, he'd keep me on the ground if the winds got too strong.

"Eep," I squealed at the sound of thunder roaring through the fields. I didn't want him to see me scared, but he gave me a quick pat on the head as he moved to the other post.

He hammered quickly, giving it one final check that the board wouldn't fall. He put the extra nails in the front pocket of his overalls. The thunder ripped through the air again, and this time lightning flashed in the distance.

"Let's head back." He held out his hand and I took it in mine. His fingers were rough as he clasped my hand, almost like the fence I had been holding.

"I'm not scared," I said.

"I know you're not," he assured me.

"Are you?"

He shook his head. "Not with a dragon rider with me. Now tell me more about this story of yours."

"Her pet dragon is a soft blue, like the sky. When she whistles, he flies down, and she gets on the saddle and rides him."

"You should name her Eleanor."

"That's my name!"

"And there's nobody else I can think of who could tame a dragon."

Poppa pulled my arm, slowing down our walk to the house. Drops of rain started to land on my head. I tried to tug on his arm, but he didn't walk any faster. "We're going to get wet," I said.

"I know," he laughed, "but that wouldn't bother a dragon rider."

The rain poured and my dress was soaked in seconds. Dad all but stopped walking. He picked me up and placed me on his shoulders. "Eleanor, the dragon rider! She's not scared of anything."

Poppa roared loudly as he started running through the yard with me on his shoulders. He held out his arms, flapping them as he flew in circles. He handed me his hammer, and I raised it high in the air, "I'm not scared of nothing!"

Chapter Twenty-Four

Skippy could see through other people's eyes. Edward's thoughts were clear, as if he spoke them aloud. He handed me a red Penny Sunday while the vendor passed him another drenched in blue syrup. He nodded to the man, handing him a dollar, and told him to keep the change.

We walked toward a bench while I used my teeth to chip away at the shaved iced. The last time I had one, I shared it with Benjie. A carnival had come to a nearby town and Poppa took us, splurging by buying far more sweets than he should. The booger's mouth had turned bright red.

"You drift off. One moment I hear you, and then, it's like you're a hundred miles away."

I nodded. "Life has been tough."

"Because of what we're able to do?"

"Can we talk of happier things?"

He gestured for me to have a seat on the bench. We sat close enough to see the infamous Central Park carousel. Before the war, this area would be overrun with mothers, their toddlers pulling at the yolk to have a ride. Now, hundreds were reduced to dozens.

"Tell me more about Skippy. First off, that can't be his actual name?"

"Seamus," Edward laughed. "He hated when I called him Skippy."

"Then, why?"

"There is nothing funnier than an angry Irishman, of course. Back then, I lived on the streets. I attempted to influence him. I wasn't good at it, not like him. It's almost funny, I was barely a man, and he dragged me into the white room."

"Oh goodness, that must have been terrifying." I covered my face as I spoke to hide the mouth full of Penny Sunday.

"I pissed myself."

The ice flew from my mouth as I laughed. Susan Lee would have been appalled at the lack of decorum. Thankfully, Edward joined in laughing. No, not laughing, snorting to the point he almost sounded like a pig. He wiped the tears from his eyes, trying to calm himself.

"Laugh all you want. But I took it easy on you. Imagine standing in that alley and I hurled you into the white room."

"You'd have done no such thing." But truth of the matter, he could have. I had no way of knowing if I could resist a telepath. I nearly confessed. Part of me wanted to explain I wasn't like him. Something in my gut held tight, refusing to tell him about the ghosts.

"I spent a year with him. Ultimately, I could influence almost as well as him. We had that in common. I can speak to other people and hear their thoughts. It was dreadful before I learned how to stop it. Skippy could see through people's eyes."

"This is fascinating." It was, and I could have listened to him talk about how he learned to control his abilities all day. Unlike me, he had no qualms talking about what he could and couldn't do.

"Have you ever met others like us?"

"Just you and Skippy. But I assume there are more. But how would we know? It's not like we can see each other use our abilities. Well," he chomped down a mouthful of ice, "except for you."

"I see through my ghost's eyes sometimes," I admitted. "It sounds kind of like what Skippy could do. But I can't do it all the time. It's a bit random."

His hand slid over mine. Beneath my palm, the coarse wood threatened to give me a nasty splinter. I didn't want to move it, not with his fingers rubbing mine. I took a bite of the shaved ice, anything to distract myself from the growing heat in my face. The base of my head ached as brain freeze set in.

"Ouch," he said, "you don't need to share everything with me."

"Serves you right for snooping around." He could only hear the loudest of my thoughts. The intimate form of communication had its perks, but something about another person knowing my every thought worried me. I was thankful to find out his telepathy had limits.

"Have you ever been on the carousel?"

Down a little path stood a large brick building composed of grand arches. It held an old carousel inside, that played obnoxiously loud music when turned on. Since we arrived at the park, we hadn't heard the song, and I wondered if it didn't work?

"I can't say I have."

"You know you're not a real New Yorker until you've been on it."

"Is that so?"

"It's a rule," he got to his feet and dramatically placed a hand over his heart, "I swear on my life."

"When did you become the mayor?"

He laughed. Despite seeing him naked in the white room, and the sex in the locker room, I blushed when he held out his hand. Edward's devilish grin would get me into trouble. The way he cocked his head to one side, showing the dimple on his face, made my heart race.

"So be it." He walked close enough our bodies continued to bump, but he made no move to hold my hand like a proper gentleman. I had to hide my amusement. For all his bravado, I made him nervous.

Edward, you can hold my hand.

For a moment, I didn't think he heard my thoughts. Without any semblance of grace, he took my hand and pulled me along. Down a small path and around to the other side of the building, we reached the gate to the carousel.

A young man with a broom swept near the entrance. I pointed at the "Closed" sign hanging from a chain that barred our entrance. "There will always be a next time."

Other than a slight tightness of his hand, Edward did nothing to respond. The man stopped cleaning, awkwardly bent over with his broom in mid-sweep. I didn't need to hear to know Edward's influence infiltrated the mind of the custodian.

"Come right in," he said. He dropped the broom and reached for the chain, unclasping it. With a grand sweeping gesture, he invited us onto the ride.

"You didn't have to do that."

"Maybe not," he said, "but I promised you a ride."

With a slight bow, I walked the short distance to the platform. Circling around the outside, there were dozens of colorful horses. Upon closer inspection, each of them was hand-painted. Time and time again artisans stopped the ride to touch up the failing paint, restoring the horses to their original vibrancy. It was silly, but I wandered between them, letting my fingers graze each of them as I looked for the perfect steed.

"This one." My fingers danced over the saddle of a horse with bright fiery red hair brighter than his pick. His choice made no sense. Neither the saddle nor the horse had been recently painted, and even one of the legs seemed to have broken off.

"And why this horse?"

"The mane." Its luscious hair was chipped in several spots. Rare were the times I focused on the aesthetics, but every little girl imagines a horse meant for just her. I was about to concede when I caught myself. No, I'd never let my light dim for the sake of a man.

"I don't—"

"It matches your dress the night we met." He spoke with such glee. The powder-blue hair had seen better days. With the bruises under my clothes, the same could be said about me. Edward didn't know it, but the color had always been my favorite, a faint memory of Momma's church dress.

"Did I say something wrong?"

It must be difficult for him finding the one person capable of concealing their thoughts. The insecurities were adorable, but so were his efforts. Never had I met somebody who recalled the color of the dress I wore the first time we met.

I leaned in and gave him a kiss. "It's perfect." I threw my leg over the back and slid into the saddle. I gripped the pole in front of me as Edward mounted his valiant steed.

"Turn it on," he said. The man who allowed us entry walked to the control booth. He wore a delightful smile on his face. I didn't know if that came about from Edward or if he was a genuinely happy person.

The music roared to life, almost too loud to bear. For a moment, I heard Poppa's voice as he told me to hang onto the pole. I did. With a jerk, the ride moved forward and off we were. My horse rose up and down as we spun around on the platform. I put away the uncomfortable memories and watched Edward smile.

I blushed. It had been ages since I found a man who captured my attention and proved to be more than a pigheaded buffoon. And yet, this one made me choke up and turn red whenever I caught his admiring eye. I didn't want the day to end, not while I spent it with him. I couldn't help but laugh. A few days ago, I would have scowled at the idea. Here I was, smitten with a man.

Not knowing my thoughts made him nervous. I didn't need to be a telepath to know. It only seemed fitting that I made him uncomfortable. He turned about, checking over his shoulder, and I gladly put my glee on display. I hugged the pole with it pressed against the side of my face, I mouthed a "Thank you."

Your welcome, he whispered.

Ironically, I tried not to dwell on the future, but I could indeed get used to this.

"What are we doing here?"

For the last hour we discussed absolutely nothing of importance. His favorite color happened to be blue, but a dark and brooding shade. It struck me as fitting. He didn't like salt on his food. He rarely drank, unless there was a need for celebration. And for some reason, he preferred New York winters over the sweltering summers. Each discussion held a playful give and take. At some point, I needed to ask Susan Lee if this is how a date should go.

However, the conversation quieted as we reached Grand Central

Station. The exterior of the building housed massive windows with columns rising from the second floor upward. Even from the exterior, it was a landmark rarely considered in the tour of New York. The last time I had been here, Frank had stolen me away from the hospital. For me, this is where my adventure in the city began.

"You like the park because there are fewer people, right? Fewer ghosts?"

I raised an eyebrow. "Yes."

"Eleanor Bouvier, it's time we step into the wilds of New York. Skippy said the best way to learn how to swim is to jump in the deep end."

"Skippy sounds like a buffoon." Our incredibly regular walk from the park had been a set-up. It was irrational, I knew it the moment I thought it, but I felt cheated. I wanted a bit of normalcy, a chance to get to know a man, not a mentalist.

"You're not happy with me?"

"Edward, you've gone and spoiled a perfectly normal day."

But we're not normal. We're more than normal. He spoke the words directly in my head as if to accentuate his point. I couldn't argue with him, but I still didn't like being tricked.

"You can be upset, I won't be offended. But I want to show you that this is part of who we are. You're trying to be one of them." He cupped my hand, squeezing it between his palms. "We're not like them."

His hands were warm, bordering on clammy. Claudette lived among people, partaking in their lives as a healer. The man I saw killed appeared like every other person. Did Edward have a point? I tried to imagine how the conversation would unfold if I told Susan Lee. It'd start with disbelief, but could she accept my abilities? Or would she pray for God to banish the demons that plagued me?

"I don't know," I admitted.

Edward's jaw clenched tight, his eyes closed. The strain worked its way through his body until his hands tightened about mine. I knew he used his gifts, but I had never seen him struggle before. Whatever he attempted, it was on a grander scale than manipulating mobsters.

"Look," he said, glancing to the side.

I gasped. The dozen people closest to us slowed their walk until they stood still. Other than an occasional car passing by, motion stopped. A woman held her son's hand, while two men were in mid-discussion. It was both amazing and terrifying. I turned back to him to see his lip quivering. With an audible exhale, the people continued walking as if nothing had changed.

"We are different, Eleanor."

"Fine."

Without hesitating, he dragged me into the train station. The inside was bigger than I remembered. The massive dome ceiling stretched the length of the building, making it a spectacle for any who entered. There were hundreds of people going to and from work. The station acted like a hub, bringing commuters into the city and allowing them to escape to the suburbs once they finished for the day. If it were not for the war, its numbers would be in the thousands.

"Do you see them?"

I shook my head. "Can you hear them all?"

He nodded. "It's like a radio between stations. There are so many I can't hear individual words. It's loud."

"Sounds dreadful."

"It sounds like New York. Now for you."

I waited for a moment, expecting them to appear at any moment on their own. The ghosts didn't need my prodding, not usually. With this, all these people there might be thousands of ghosts, and they'd overlap until the station transformed into a sea of transparent residents. It'd be impossible to tell who each belonged to.

Edward moved behind me and held me by my hips. "Light the match."

I closed my eyes and imagined both of my hands cupped at chest height. Pushing at the flame, I imagined it glowing softly in my hands. I knew the moment the light appeared, it wasn't the real fire Edward wanted. Focusing, I shook my imaginary hands and brought them together again. I tried again and the tiny flame sprang to life. Something inside me knew it wasn't the same.

"I can't."

"The woman betting on boxing matches and facing mobsters doesn't know the meaning of the word, 'can't,' does she?"

I opened my eyes and saw several ghosts in the space. They came of their own accord. I didn't want them to magically appear on their own. I wanted to summon them and extinguish the fire when I commanded it. Closing my eyes again, I pushed the anger into my hands. The match struck and the tiniest of fires ignited. It wasn't enough to not consider myself a master.

Every time Momma told me to stop speaking with the devil, and my Poppa held me when the demons scared me, each emotion traveled down my arms. Pooling in my hand like gasoline, the spark turned into a blaze. It dripped from my hands. I opened my eyes.

Thousands.

Every man, woman, and child had hundreds of ghosts. From a split second to minutes into their future, I could see their destinies unfold. I didn't think I'd be able to trace the specters back to their owners, but it proved an easier task than I predicted. The opaque residents froze as a moment stretched on for eternity.

I focused on a man in a suit holding a briefcase. Only a dozen feet away, I followed his future as he reached the platform and boarded the train. It played out as I looked through his eyes. The station remained unmoving, but part of my me watched as he read the newspaper. When the conductor approached his seat, they would exchange money and the man in the blue moved on.

I traveled with the ticket taker, going from seat to seat. The train shifted, and we traveled away from the station. I had only ever jumped from ghosts once before. If I maintained my focus, could I continue seeing the futures of every person on the train? Did I have to move between adjacent ghosts or could I choose my path at random?

The moment I lost my concentration, drowning in a sea of hypotheticals, I snapped back to my body. Time resumed and opaque figures moved into their future selves. I closed my eyes and pressed my hands together, squashing the flame. I took a moment before opening my eyes to see a massive room only occupied by the present.

"It worked," I whispered.

159

"We're not normal," he repeated, "we're amazing."

I couldn't argue with his logic.

Just like my bedroom, the paint along the ceiling hung on for dear life. A chip drifted downward, landing at the foot of the bed. In the daylight, the entire apartment appeared as if it was well on its way to being deemed uninhabitable. Water stains browned the walls, and more than one window had a missing pane. As I swung my feet about, I could feel the uneven floorboards beneath my toes.

I ached in a way only achievable by a night of vigorous lovemaking. My thighs still burned and my right nipple stung as I moved. I knew I'd pay for it in the morning. It was more than exciting getting to this point. Edward had his shortcomings, but his generosity in bed would leave me spoiled for future suitors.

"I can almost hear you," he mumbled. The moment I spotted the grin, I was sure he picked up on the endearing parts. He might have ravished me the night before, but the self-satisfied expression written across his face reminded me he was far from perfect.

"Stop trying to see inside my head."

"I've already seen everywhere else." Smug. It was charming, to a point that is. I had to admit, sex with a mentalist was unlike anything I had experienced before. It was like being caught between two places, one that intensified the emotional side while the other remained quite carnal. I'm certain I'd never experience something that satisfying with a normal man.

"I need to get dressed." In the afternoon sun, it was almost embarrassing hunting for my underwear, trying to remember where he removed them. I found my stockings and a wayward shoe, but panties seemed nowhere—

"I believe you might want these?" Edward scooted off the bed, raising my underwear from his side of the bed. The saunter of his walk gave away just how impressed he was with himself. I nearly gulped as I caught sight of his manhood fully erect. I worried my imagination may have inflated the memory. It had not, not even a little.

"Are you sure you need to be going?"

Something in my stomach tightened at the thought of his skill in bed. He knew I wanted it. He simply wasn't used to a woman resisting his charm.

"Unfortunately for you, yes. I have business that needs attending." He pouted. Without his telepathy, he had to rely on his boyish good looks. It made me wonder how regularly he used his abilities to persuade lovers.

"Surely, it can wait?"

"How often do women tell you no?" Other than our abilities, I wasn't entirely sure how much we had in common. For all I knew, Edward might be far more free with his morals.

"It has been known to happen from time to time."

"Do you ever influence them?"

He paused at the question. I may very well be the only woman capable of resisting his abilities. It was uncharted territory for him as much as it was for me. There was a moment where I could tell he pondered lying. I hid my surprise when he opted for the truth.

"It has happened."

The ramifications of that statement... Did this constitute as rape? Did he simply stroke the embers, already burning in the women? I knew I should leave it alone, but I needed to hear the whole truth.

"Do you bed them against their will?"

He tossed my underwear to me. The conversation had visibly stolen the thunder from his manhood. I knew I was walking the wire between curiosity and offense.

"You mean, do I force them?"

"Is that how you see it?" His next statement would draw a line in the sand, and I wasn't quite sure if we'd be standing on the same side.

"No, and no. I've never needed to influence them against their will." If he had stopped there, we might have ended this encounter on a satisfying note. "They're not like us, Eleanor. We are something more than human. We do things they've only dreamed of."

"You think these abilities put us above right and wrong?"

He had to consider it for a moment. "Yes, matter of fact, I do. We can do these things, these absolutely amazing things. Why should we be limited by the rules they've created for themselves?"

"You're not talking about simply stealing from the rich or influencing gamblers while betting. You're talking about robbing them of choice. We're not gods."

"Aren't we, though?"

I wasn't willing to get into a debate, not with Edward, and definitely not about the wrongness of that statement. I slipped my underwear on, shaking my head.

"No," I slid my dress over my head. "We are anything but."

"You can't possibly believe that? You use your abilities to get what you want just as much as I do."

I had to admit, there was a sense of entitlement. The world had robbed me of so much, and at any moment, I felt as if I could steal it back, to rally against fate and demand what it owed. The urge laid just beneath the surface, but it was a quiet voice I silenced. Whether a curse or a gift, I wanted to utilize these abilities to make a difference, to put forth good into the universe.

"It's there," I admitted, "but there are lines I refuse to cross."

"That might be the difference between you and me." His voice remained calm, almost disappointed that I refused to be a queen ruling at his side. My heart sank just as much as his. This could be the conversation that would inevitably doom our chances of something long term.

"I guess it is."

I slipped on my shoes and walked across the room, careful not to trip on the broken floor. Offering a sullen smile, I pulled the door open.

Goodbye. Even in his thoughts, I heard the melancholy. I would have almost preferred shouting at one another. The calm manner in which he spoke struck me harder. I parted without a farewell. It was a conversation that could wait until after I stopped a killer.

Chapter Twenty-Five

New York had a distinct smell when it rained. The notes of life and exuberance gave way to hints of horror and fear. When the rain invaded New York, her citizens hid in their homes and the streets appeared almost empty. Normally I thought of the rain as refreshing, washing away the grime, but tonight, it set the mood. Dark swirling clouds loomed overhead, bad omens warning me against whatever rash action I was about to take. Lightning lit up the sky, revealing the darkness of shadows as they retreated. The thunder grumbled, not yet ready to unleash its booming bass.

The storm should have been a sign.

I hadn't been waiting long before the water saturated my clothes, leaving them damp and me shivering. If I had been prepared, I might've brought an umbrella or a plastic wrap to drape over my shoulders. Sheer stubbornness would get me through the night. I just hoped that I didn't die from pneumonia in the process.

If I had truly thought out a plan, I might have stolen Frank's gun, or a bat, or something. At least Vincent had loaned me a pocket-sized weapon. I had to wonder if I was being careless by taking such a monumental risk. Was this to prove myself capable or to prove myself invulnerable? The more I dwelled on it, the less I liked the answer. Once I stopped the killer, I'd harness a bit of Susan Lee's optimism and put my abilities to work for a greater good.

The buildings about this block were all three stories high with flat roofs. Across the street from the shop, looking down, I could see all the entrances into the wide alley housing Claudette's business. I didn't dare wait in the alley, fearful the man in the bomber jacket might somehow creep up behind me. From my perch there were only two points of entry, the stairwell inside the building and the fire escape.

I glanced over my shoulder, checking the rooftop door again. Wedged between the handle and the ground was a thick metal pipe. Even if he opened the door, I'd hear the clink of the pipe against the roof. The only other way to reach me was the fire escape. He would have to jump up and grab the ladder and climb three stories. Here, I was safe to be a watchful vigilante.

How long would it take? I could do this for an evening, perhaps two, but after a while, Susan Lee would start asking questions. I could reach inside and ignite the flame and call on the ghosts. The roof would fill with lovers escaping their parents or sneaking a fag late at night. The alley below could reveal hundreds of ghosts, but I feared what they might show me. Not knowing meant the future wasn't written, but the moment they revealed the timeline, Father Time etched destiny into stone.

Being alone and caught in the storm gave me a chance to reflect on my disagreement with Edward. I continued holding back the nature of the ghosts. Lies begot more lies, and lying was something I had a knack for. Revealing the truth, the *entire* truth, that was something I had only done with two men in my life. Edward might send my stomach into knots each time I saw him, but did I trust him as much as my father or Frank? Obviously not.

I might not care for some of his less scrupulous methods of living, or his insistence he was owed a bit of slack because of his childhood. I couldn't lose him, the only person who knew me, or *could*, someday.

Edward, I'm sorry. I yelled the thought in my head, hoping it reached him. I had never been in a fight with a telepath before. Could he hear me and still ignore me? Was there a barrier separating us? When the light broke, I'd find my way to his apartment and maybe fill in the gaps in my story.

Lightning flashed across the sky, revealing the tallest buildings of New York in the distance. The rain intensified as the thunder shook the air. The rain fell in sheets. I hadn't expected much when I decided to be a hero. There was no thanks needed. I didn't want recognition. But I hadn't anticipated being a hero involved a world of boredom. Being a hero was less punching than I hoped.

Hours passed and the clock must have neared midnight. I leaned against the wall surrounding the roof, peering into the street below. With buckets of water tearing their way through the alley, I found it difficult to see more than a lamp struggling to ward away the darkness. I held my hand to my eyes, blocking the rain, squinting into the shadows at the far end of the shop. Paranoia had set in as I stared at a black shape I was convinced was moving.

Lightning flashed again. I froze as a figure came into view. He worked his way down the street, careful to stay in the shadows. As he approached Claudette's door, he paused, looking up and down the alley. I dropped low as he scanned the tops of the buildings.

I hadn't considered how he found his prey. If he detected mentalists, he might already know I watched. I couldn't spook him, or I'd never make it down the fire escape fast enough to catch him before he ran back to the street. If the killer could detect me, he didn't seem to care as he walked toward the door of Claudette's shop.

The moment he disappeared under the canopy, I burst into action. I climbed down the ladder, jumping down the last few rungs to the landing. Boots had been the smart choice as I spun around the stairs and descended to the second floor. The metal grates under my feet kept me from slipping, but if I wasn't careful, I'd snap my neck before I got to the killer.

As I reached the ladder that'd take me to the street, I paused to see if the killer had gone inside. The door to Claudette's shop was open, flapping in the breeze. She'd most likely be in her apartment at the back of the shop. I hoped she had reinforced the door to prepare.

I hadn't been sure he'd return, but after seeing his ferocity in my vision, I couldn't imagine him walking away until he completed his mission.

Reaching the bottom of the ladder, I shoved down with all my weight. It slid a few feet, leaving me a four-foot drop. I risked the sprained ankle, bending my knees as I landed, absorbing the impact. I reached into my pocket, pulling out Vincent's brass knuckles, the only weapon I had the foresight of bring with me. It wasn't flashy, but it'd get the job done.

There was no point in hiding. If the man could detect my presence, my footsteps would be the least of my worries. If he was a mentalist hunting his own kind, I was about to walk into this fight practically unarmed. My abilities served me in the boxing ring, giving me just enough of an edge to win a fight. It was time to summon the ghosts.

The imaginary scene remained the same as before. My hand hovered in front of me, palm up, ready to cradle the flame. The hand in my mind flicked its wrist, and I expected the tiny flicker to appear. Whether it was nerves or the logic of actual falling rain, I couldn't summon the fire.

"Eleanor, child, is that you?"

Claudette stood in the doorway of her shop, clutching a shawl draped over her shoulders. She appeared confused as to why I was standing in the deluge, ready to storm into her shop in the dead of night. If the killer hadn't gone in to find her, it meant he was still in the alley.

"Shit."

Chapter Twenty-Six

"Go inside! Lock the door. Call the cops," I shouted.

"What's goi—"

The rain pelting against the pavement made it impossible to know how he approached. He used the deluge to his advantage. Relying on brute force and determination with the others, I had earned his stealth and cunning. He wasn't as smart as he believed.

If I turned and punched, he'd slash at my arms. If I ducked, I exposed my neck, even an elbow back left my legs open. Instead, I did the unpredictable; I dove forward. The pavement hurt as I slid, tiny rocks cutting into my hands. I spun over and saw him pause. I knew I had made the right move.

Scurrying to my feet, I readied to meet him head-on. He wielded the razor like before. I understood why Claudette called him a thing. There was nothing but a single drive. She mentioned her people making zombis. Was he one of them?

I didn't have long to ponder as he charged, arm pulled back. He'd attempt to drag it along my torso, if I blocked, he'd catch my forearm. There would be words later as I ignored Frank's lessons and stepped into the man, too close for him to swing the blade. I grabbed his arm by the elbow with my left hand, making it impossible for him to reach me. I took the easy jab, brass knuckles braced in my hand. The crack across his face sounded like thunder, bone crumbling just below his eye.

He clutched my throat with his free hand. He shoved me backward, forcing my back toward the alley wall. I let him guide me, surrendering my only escape. I wanted him to think I had no place to run. What I needed was something to brace myself.

I refused to release his arm as he tried to shake my grip. The moment my grip loosened, he'd have a clear swipe at my throat. I put my right foot against the wall and used his arm as leverage, lifting myself up. I pushed off and cracked a fist against his collar bone, using my body weight to knock him back.

The blow to the face and then the shoulder would have sent a man into the shadows to lick his wounds. The master pulling at his strings had been specific—kill. He might try to push his way past my guard again, but he narrowed his gait, appearing more like the boxers in the ring than he had the first time we met.

"I've whopped bigger men than you," I hissed. I did the same, leading with my left fist, keeping my hands high enough to protect my throat. Frank would be proud that I finally listened.

He acted as if he would lead with his fist and ignore me with the blade. I could see the weight resting on the wrong foot, giving away the feigning tactic. He'd draw back to lure me in, and then the razor would tear through the fabric of my shirt and into the muscle of my forearms.

I tried to feign a punch, hoping he'd start swinging and I could grip his wrist and land a solid uppercut to the face. He might not be the most skilled, but he knew enough to switch his weight quickly, leaving me unsure of his approach. He jabbed wildly, and I leaned to the side to avoid the blow.

The blade in his hand flashed, and I spotted my error. He wasn't attempting to box. He wanted to finish the fight. Unlike him, I couldn't absorb blows left and right and stay on my feet. The underhand cut caught my thigh, slipping through the fabric and slicing into my flesh. He tried to change directions and catch my torso, but I pivoted on my foot, pulling out of his reach.

Did he sever something important? Was this the blow that ended the attack? I feared I might bleed out if I didn't get medical attention quickly. I could put weight on my leg, but the injury forced out a howl. We circled one another. I growled, trying to push away the pain before it removed me from the fight.

My patience waned as I waited for him to make his move. Leaning in, I put all my weight on the ball of my left foot. Instead of following through with a punch, I swung my leg. My toe connecting with his torso, while I grabbed the wrist of his blade hand. Before I could retract the limb, he trapped it with his arm, pinning it to his side.

He fought to free the hand holding the razor. I didn't have time to think, he'd flay my leg once he shook me. I bounced up with my other leg and kicked. My heel nailed him in the gut. As he stumbled back, the razor skipped along the flesh next to my thumb. I landed on my back with an oomph, the wind thrust from my lungs.

He regrouped faster than me. I had a flashback to yesterday morning. Being on my back robbed me of any chance of defeating him. A cloth fell around his head, stopping him cold. Claudette grunted behind him, her shawl tightening about his neck. It was the second time she had saved my life.

I needed to return the favor.

Before I got to my feet, the killer had spun about, slicing Claudette along her torso, deep enough that she screamed and let go. I feared my vision was coming true, and this was the start of the end for the woman.

From my crouching position, I lunged. I barreled into the killer, my arms around his chest. We sailed past Claudette. The moment he struck the cement, I brought back my hand, clubbing him in the back of the head with the brass knuckles. My first blow stopped him from struggling to turn over. The second made his body go limp.

I smashed him three more times before I realized the rain couldn't wash the blood off my fist fast enough. Stopping the killer hadn't been adequate, I had beaten him to death with my own two hands. I wasn't sure my heart had any remorse.

I flipped my soggy hair behind me to see Claudette's face.

Clutching her side with both hands, she couldn't hide her horror. I had promised to stop the killer. I said I would do it at any cost. The price was too much for her. I could tell she feared the ferocity. Did she think I was as bad as the man on the ground?

"It was us or him." Standing over the dead man, I waited for lighting to see the damage. As the sky flashed, it revealed the side of his skull collapsed inward. I removed the brass knuckles, the palm of my hand sore from the grip. "Claudette. Him or us."

She didn't respond immediately. Another flash of lightning illuminated the alley. Whatever thoughts were being processed in her head came to an end. She jumped into action. Bending down and picking up the blade, she handed it to me. "Hold that."

Claudette hissed as she moved, checking the red stain bleeding down her shirt. The woman lifted the man by the hand, dragging him toward the door to her shop. "We need evidence before the rain destroys it."

I pocketed the razor and grabbed the other arm. We pulled, lugging the corpse to the door. The light of the shop struggled to penetrate the sheets of rain. But now I could make out his head. I hadn't beaten him until he stopped moving, I had pulverized his skull.

Black bits wedged under my fingernails. I let go of the body while Claudette continued dragging him inside. Scrubbing my skin with my blouse, I attempted to get the man's blood off me. I couldn't tell if it worked, but I scraped until I was sure I had given myself rug burn.

Claudette dropped the man. As she stepped away, I let out an audible gasp. Lying on the floor, the killer occupied the spot where the chalk would eventually be drawn.

"He's the body," I whispered, satisfied with my handiwork.

I leaned against the doorway, exhausted and fearful I might topple over. "I saved them," For the first time, I thought the universe took pity on me.

Claudette peeled away her shirt, inspecting the wound on her torso. "It hurts worse than it is. Let's get a look at you."

"I'm a hero." I couldn't help but laugh as the world grew dark.

Claudette's living room was exactly as I pictured it. Her walls bared artwork from around the world and several medical textbooks rested on her shelves. There was no radio and no phone. With the light diffused through a scarf, it added warmth to the space. There was little out of place, but a thin layer of dust suggested she wasn't one to sweat the details.

"What happened?" I asked, pulling a cool cloth from my forehead. "I don't remember…" I could recall the fight, but after, the world got blurry. I assumed Claudette took care of me. At this rate, I'd owe her a lifetime of favors.

"In the shop," came a voice.

I slowly pushed myself upright, and everything spun. I closed my eyes, and the moment I did, I could sense the pain in my leg. I pulled the knitted blanket away to see she had removed my pants and bandaged my leg. The tinted goop Claudette used on cuts was applied haphazardly. I'd have to introduce the healer to Susan Lee to learn how to properly dress a wound.

I eased my way to my feet, making sure I had a firm grip on the couch arm with my good hand. The room seemed uneven as I took my first step. A steadying breath helped push away the nausea, but it didn't prevent the room from tilting under my feet. I braced myself on the wall, letting it support my weight as I found my way to the door into the shop.

Claudette stood upright, shirtless, as she applied a bandage to her torso. Susan Lee would gasp at the application. The thought made me grin. Grinning hurt.

Outside, thunder boomed, the storm persisting. I had to wonder how long I had been out. "What time is it?"

"It's almost three. How is your head, child?"

If I ignored it, it'd go away. Being stubborn was a necessary trait in the ring, and I hoped I could continue the brave face until I made my way home. "It'll be fine."

"It worried me he broke something. My remedies can only do so much. You'll have a nasty scar on your leg, but you'll live."

"It wasn't you," I said as I stepped through the door and bumped against the counter. I braced myself, leaning over far enough to see feet sticking out on the other side. "The chalk outline. It wasn't you. I was wrong."

She thought about it for a moment, looking from the dead man on the floor to me. "There are no mistakes, child. You saw the signs of death and feared it was me. Without that fear, would you have been hiding across the street waiting for him?"

I thought about the string of logic. "Probably not."

"You didn't misinterpret them, you just didn't realize the entire picture. They guided you here."

Even when the future didn't show me a clear picture, it still tortured me. I shimmied around the counter to the man and the puddle of blood collecting around his skull. My heart thumped in my chest, but I couldn't detect remorse.

"Did you find any clues?"

The frown answered the question for me. She gestured with her chin to the body. "There was nothing on him. No personal items, but he does have a single tattoo. He is as average as they come. I found scars on his chest, though."

I didn't want to touch a dead body, but I needed every clue I could get. Why did he seek out mentalists, and who did he call master?

A quarter-sized patch of stubble grew near his temple, meaning he shaved his head, further washing away his identity. The pale skin and slender facial features made it nearly impossible to remember him. The only identifying trait was the smile and jacket. Unsnapping the breast of his coat, he wore a standard white shirt you'd find under a button-down shirt. Nothing about him appeared unique, just an anonymous killer.

I lifted his shirt, looking for the tattoo, hoping it might help identify the man. Lifting it high enough to see his collar bone, the only thing that adorned his unremarkable body were hundreds of thin scars. Even the bullet wound from Claudette seemed to be missing. I touched the raised bits of flesh, hoping I'd catch a glimpse of the future. Nothing, just rough strips of skin.

"Razor-blade scars," I mumbled.

"I agree. It looks like someone had cut him a hundred times," she added.

"Fighting perhaps? Or maybe it is some part of an initiation. Where's the tattoo?"

"Hip closest to you."

Did Claudette undress the man and put his clothes back on? I looked to his waistband and found the tip of the tattoo, and with a slight tug, I could see the three wavy lines.

"It's a brand," Claudette said. "Whoever branded him, they wanted it clear who owned him." I shivered at the idea of being nothing more than property.

"I've seen this before," I mumbled as I touched the symbol. His skin was still damp, clammy to the touch. I'd kill him a second time if it was required, but I didn't want to spend more time with the corpse than I had to. The symbol was simple enough; I didn't need a sketch to remember.

I leaned in close to the cuts on the chest. There was no scent to the man, just the wet New York smell. I couldn't detect cologne or body odor. Even my senses believed he didn't exist. I touched the scars to verify they were created years ago.

"I need to call the police," Claudette said. "It is best you aren't here. Let them believe he attempted to rob me for medical supplies."

I ignored her.

"What are these?" On his neck I could see a series of tiny black dots. I touched them, but the water on my finger made it impossible to feel if they were raised or indents in the skin. Susan Lee would be proud. "He has needle punctures in his neck. Somebody drugged the man..."

"Zombi," Claudette mumbled.

"Call the cops," I said. I needed to speak with Edward, let him know the threat was over. I'd sleep better tonight knowing the killer was dead. Between Susan Lee and Edward, I might be able to piece together the needle marks and the symbol on his hip.

"I'm glad you're alive."

"I still have a role to play, child. Be gone. Be safe. I'll consult the

Loa and see if they will grant me eyes to see the bigger picture." She handed me a skirt that I pulled up around my waist. I was hobbling out the door as she picked up the phone.

"Police," she said in a terror-stricken voice, "I think I killed a man..."

Chapter Twenty-Seven

The smell of sulphur filled the air as I struck a match. Carefully shielding the fire, I let it jump from the wood stick to the wick of the candle. Our bedroom seemed even more frightening with the shadows clawing their way up, stretching into sight. I waited for a moment, expecting Benjie to spring from his hiding place to scare me, but the familiar roar never came.

"Hello?" I called out to the shadows. Thankfully, none replied.

I lifted the candle and walked to the bedroom door, my hand trembling as it rested on the knob. It turned slowly, as I prepared at any moment to jump into the air with a slight screech. The door crept open, but the little booger was nowhere to be found. The hallway connecting the bedrooms was vacant except for the dancing shadows along the wall.

"Benjie, this isn't funny."

I assumed he had escaped in the middle of the night and crawled under the covers with Momma. Since the military man had come for Poppa, the booger spent more time sleeping with her than with me. I liked having the entire bed to myself, but Momma had given me strict orders to keep him in our room. He spent all day under her skirt, and I guessed she wanted to sleep in peace.

Tiptoeing down the hall, the floorboards whined as I worked my way toward Poppa and Momma's bedroom. I slipped inside, listening quietly for the sound of Benjie's familiar whimpers. Nightmares made him flop around at night, and I often woke as he kicked me or a hand smacked against my face. The covers to the bed were on the floor, but neither Benjie nor Momma was anywhere to be found.

I froze as a white figure stepped into the middle of the room. At first, I thought it might be Momma in a nightgown, but it blinked in and out of sight. A chill spread along my skin as the ghost walked toward and through me. I tried not to move, hoping it wouldn't come back and touch me again. The ghost moved toward the stairs and vanished. I refused to be scared, or at least not to cry out for Momma to come save me. I was a warrior. I wasn't terrified of no ghosts.

The shutters outside Momma's room rattled as the winds threaten to break them free. There was a storm brewing, a potential tornado, the third this month. I ran back into the hallway before peeking down the stairs. There were no ghosts, just another dark, empty space. I moved the candle to my left hand, careful not to drip wax on the floor. Down the stairs I went, each step groaning.

I glimpsed the white ghost standing at the front door. She stood at the door for a moment before inviting in a second ghost. This one was a tall man wearing a uniform like the one Poppa wore. Ghosts lived in these walls, horrific demons trying to trick me all the time. Now the ghost of Momma invited more into the house. I wanted to ask why they weren't in Heaven or why they stayed at the farm.

"Momma," I called out quietly. There was no response. The floors did not creek as the two ghosts walked into the living room. I wouldn't be scared. They were just ghosts, they couldn't hurt me. I needed to know why they were here. Did they live here? Were we the ones living in their house?

I worked my way closer to the front door until I could see them in the living room. Momma sat in a chair while the man sat on the couch opposite her. His lips were moving, but I couldn't hear what he was saying. I would make them go away and protect Momma and Benjie. I wouldn't be mean, but they couldn't live here with us.

"Hello?" I asked, but either they didn't hear, or they ignored me.

The gentleman had his hat sitting in his lap, looking very formal. I had seen Poppa in his uniform the morning he returned to the army. The man on the couch looked more serious, his lips pursed in that way Momma did when she got sad.

I saw through the man to the quilt she draped on the back of the couch to hide a hole Benjie made. I waited for him to look up as I stepped from the stairs, but he acted like I wasn't there. Could ghosts not hear me like I couldn't hear them? His lips moved as if he spoke to the ghost of Momma, except nothing came out. But I could see her head bobbing before she folded over, her head hidden by the chair.

"Are you all right, Momma?"

He scooted to the edge of the couch and rested a hand on her back. I stepped into the living room while they remained unaware of me. Momma held a piece of paper in her head as her body heaved. I had never seen her cry before. The sight made my chest hurt. I didn't know what to do as the tears started rolling down my eyes. Momma shouldn't be sad about anything in the world.

"Get away from her!"

The tips of my fingers passed harmlessly through his arm. I couldn't feel the fabric of his coat. The ghost didn't blow away in the wind like I hoped. Instead, he got down on one knee next to my sobbing mother and patted her softly on the back. Whatever he said, he broke Momma. By now, tears streamed down my face, partly because of seeing her cry, but also I felt useless. Poppa had told me to be strong, to be a warrior, and I couldn't save her.

The paper slipped from her hand and slid along the floor. I stepped through his arm, quick in case he noticed. Trying to grab it, I found there was nothing for me to lift. I got down on my hands and knees and tried to focus on the letters. At first it was hard to read like the individual letters were blurry or shaking. With my nose only inches away, I could make out the first few words.

"Deeply regret…"

"Ellie, you're not staying in bed with the sun shining outside." I blinked to see Momma picking Benjie's socks off the floor. She draped them over her arm as she snatched his dungarees from the post of the bed. "Go outside and play with Benjie."

"Momma?" I wiped the sleep from my eyes. "You can hear me?"

"Of course I can. How such a small girl can make so much noise sleeping is beyond me."

"Poppa?" She could hear me. It had been a horrible dream and now I was safe in my bed again. I breathed a sigh of relief.

"The mail hasn't come yet," she said as she pushed the curtains open wide. She paused for a moment. "Hmm, the sun won't be out long. It looks like a storm is coming."

The ghost stepped from my mother. I pulled the blankets high enough that only my eyes were visible. It continued picking up Benjie's clothes before walking out of the room. Momma, my real Momma, didn't see the spirit.

The ghosts were real, but they only tortured me.

Chapter Twenty-Eight

I kept my head down as I ran through the street. The rain continued its war against the grime lining the streets. Claudette's skirt had all but turned see-through, clinging to my legs. I didn't like being wet, and being wet, beaten, and hardly wearing clothes, none of this brought me joy.

Reaching my apartment building, I bound up the stairs quickly. I needed to put on reasonable clothes and find Edward. Multiple times I attempted to shout at him and he ignored me. It was as if he left his mental phone off the hook to avoid being disturbed. Our fight had been passionate, but I don't think it warranted this level of isolation.

I had to remind myself that I hardly knew the man. Perhaps this bit of childish snubbing was standard for him. If I had the ability, I'd drag him into the white room and force him to confront me face to face. I needed to see him and explain myself. Maybe he'd celebrate in my victory over the serial killer.

At the top of the stairs, resting in front of my door, was a cardboard box. I couldn't imagine what would be delivered in the middle of the night. It had a bit of heft as I tucked it under my arm. I fumbled with my keys in a rush to get out of these wretched clothes.

Off they went the moment I closed the door. I was in a hurry. A shower would have to wait. I grabbed a pair of trousers, a dark-colored blouse, and sensible boots. I didn't need to impress Edward, I just needed him to stop being pig-headed.

"Susan Lee, I blame you for my infatuation with a man." A week ago, if somebody had asked if I'd be willing to chase a boy, I'd have laughed. Now here I was, letting his neglect fuel my actions. I'd have to reflect on this when I had a moment. The last thing I needed was a reputation for being boy crazy.

Peaking in Susan Lee's room, I made sure she was working a late shift at the hospital. I changed in record time. Before leaving, I stepped in front of the mirror and admired myself, truly admired myself. On a superficial level, I was pretty, but that wasn't what struck me. For hours I had been running on adrenaline and hadn't taken a moment to state the obvious.

"I stopped a killer," I said out loud. I straightened my back and smiled at my reflection. Despite the numerous bandages and bruising starting to form, I was impressed with myself.

"I did it." It didn't feel real yet. I had set out to protect New Yorkers, and as details unfolded, my motives changed. I didn't want to protect just New Yorkers, I wanted to protect my own kind. Edward, Claudette, myself, we were unique. I couldn't let a crazy man snuff out our light before our time.

"Next, I'll stop whoever created him." It wasn't an aspirational quote I wanted to live up to. It was a fact. I had faith it would happen. The killer's body continued to make me uneasy, with the sheer lack of identity. He could have been anybody, an average nobody.

I couldn't quite put my finger on the exact moment in time, but something massive had changed in the universe. This new scary idea of hope left me wondering where my place in the world might be. After hiding from society for so long, perhaps there was a place for a woman capable of seeing the future.

I grabbed an umbrella on the way into the hall, prepared to storm out the door and apologize to Edward. I paused and looked over my shoulder to the package sitting on the kitchen table. Curiosity got the best of me, I needed to know who would leave a pristine white box on my door.

"I'm betting it's a present from Susan Lee's latest suitor."

I pulled at the twine holding it together and let out a chuckle. Despite all my raging against being one of *those* girls, I still held my breath as I opened the box. Apparently there were some things that no amount of resisting could overcome. I tore the tissue paper apart, shocked to see it was indeed a gift for me.

Lifting the leather jacket, I inspected the spots where the threads had started to come loose. Emma Jean had done an immaculate job tidying up the worn edges. I didn't have time for further inspection, and instead I slipped it on to take with me. If I would see Edward, I wanted to make sure I exuded all the confidence possible.

I locked the door and shoved the keys in my pocket, and a minute later I bound down the street, heading to Edward's apartment. The streets were empty, the residents of New York City asleep in their beds, curled up in preparation for another long day of work. I envied them. Right now, my body wanted sleep. I was running on adrenaline and stubbornness. Eventually, I'd be a sloppy lump of dead weight.

If I was lucky, it'd happen in Edward's bed.

Even with the umbrella, my shoes were soaked by the time I reached Edward's block. I don't know if the chills going through my body were the result of the rain or the developing pain in my body. The adrenaline faded, and instead of being tired, I moved from determined to achy. As I stood on the corner of his street, I contemplated turning around and going home. I wanted to be in good form, but the victory of this morning carried me forward.

Stubbornness put one foot in front of the other. In my race to change my clothes and reach his apartment, it hadn't dawned on me that he might not be home. Or, if he was, he might not open the door for me. Doubts worked their way through my armor, and each step forward slowed as I thought up a dozen reasons to turn around.

"No," I mumbled to myself.

The row of houses were worse off than my own building. Each one had a decrepit set of stairs leading up to the first floor. I hadn't asked how he'd managed to acquire it, but I could make an educated guess. It wasn't the nicest part of the city, making our own look upscale. With a few more carefully placed bets, I bet I could make up the difference—if the mob didn't kill me first.

I climbed the stairs, shaking my umbrella as I crossed the threshold. Like me, he lived on the third floor. By the second set of stairs, the cut in my leg screamed at me. I was certain, even with Claudette's magic, I'd managed to open the wound. The battle scar would require an explanation every time I wore shorts or undressed. Susan Lee would not be impressed.

His door was like every other, a worn gray in a dingy white hallway. I tried rapping my knuckles against it quietly so as not to disturb other potential residents. Patience had never, nor would it ever be a virtue. I knocked again, this time louder. If he was asleep, it was enough to force him from the bed.

"Come on, Edward," I whispered with my face against the door.

"Pssst," came a voice from down the hall. I turned to see light creeping through an ajar door. A young girl stood with her eye at the crack, the chain still fastened. It was long past her bedtime.

"There was shouting and banging hours ago. Mom said I should mind my own business. But it kept me up."

I mouthed a silent, "Thank you," to the girl. She vanished, shutting the door and the deadbolt locked into place.

I feared the mobsters had come about, looking for Edward for helping me cheat them out of money. My heart jumped in my chest, fearful that my actions had put him in danger. I wouldn't be able to forgive myself if they hurt him.

Grabbing the doorknob, I wiggled it furiously, only to find it was locked. I gave the door a slight shoulder, hoping to force it open. In our building, it might have given, but here, the doors were made to keep out the riff-raff. The door refused to budge under my weight.

I took several steps back and prepared for an aching shoulder. Leaning forward, I hurled my weight against the door, forcing the doorframe to split. Another solid blow with my shoulder and the door broke away from the frame and swung open.

I slid inside quickly, hoping to avoid nosey neighbors. Shutting it behind me, I hoped nobody was awake enough to call the cops. I'm sure Edward would normally influence them, but I didn't have that luxury. If they arrived while I was inside, there would be questions, ones I couldn't answer.

Shoes. Both rested by the doorway, untouched since I left. I had to be observant, take in the scene and—

Ghosts. Two cops with their guns drawn, inspecting the scene. I didn't know how much time remained until they showed. My eyes closed and I forced the flame to quiet, but I decided I might be able to use their detective skills to help solve the mystery.

I poked my head in the bathroom to see a towel draped over the sink. The fabric held that moist feeling, perhaps a couple of hours since he used it to dry himself.

"There was no struggle," I whispered. I imagined the list of people who wanted to kidnap Edward was lengthy. If it had been mobsters, they would have had to overwhelm him. He could influence plenty of people. Perhaps it was somebody he robbed? Something was entirely off about this situation. How did they surprise him?

"Dammit." The ghosts of the cops inspected every nook and cranny, attempting to sort out the owner of the apartment.

The bed hadn't been disturbed since I left. He had taken a shower, perhaps getting ready to call it a night. He would have gotten himself a glass of water from the kitchen. No, he'd want a nightcap. I elbowed the door as I bust into the room he treated as his study. A single chair faced a wall with a world map. He had driven pins into the locations he wanted to visit once he had the funds.

The officer pointed at the glass of whiskey, nudging it with his pistol. The amber liquid inside had barely dipped below two fingers. His bragging about the cost of the liquid meant he'd never leave a drop in the glass before going to bed.

The small square table was bare except for the glass tumbler. I pushed it to the side like the cop had. I gasped. Three wavy lines had been carved through the table's varnish. The same symbol as the killer's tattoo who attacked Claudette. Had he come here before going after her?

"Edward has been taken. He would have been unconscious, there's no way he'd leave without his shoes. The killer would have had to carry him out. But where could he have gone before attacking Claudette?"

The second officer called over his partner. I watched as they talked about something they saw on the far side of the chair. Stepping around the table, I could see the collection of wallets Edward had liberated. There must have been at least twenty, still folded but most likely free of their money.

The smell of whiskey hit my nose. I hadn't had a drink since—

"Oh, no." The whiskey. The wavy lines, they matched the embossing from the leather book. All clues pointed to Susan Lee's doctor friend. I had no idea why the man hunted mentalists, or why he'd kidnap Edward instead of killing him. But at least I had a lead, and I knew exactly where to find answers.

"Hello," came a voice from the front door. I nearly jumped at the break in the silence. I opened the window, climbing onto the fire escape. There was no way I could explain to the cops why I had broken in, or that a killer had kidnapped Edward. If I wound up handcuffed in the back of their car, I might not be able to make it in time.

I slipped out the window, back into the rain, lowering it gently behind me. I moved down the fire escape, working my way to the alley below. Within the hour, this madness would come to an end.

First, save Edward, then get answers.

Chapter Twenty-Nine

My emotions fluctuated wildly. Somewhere between fearing for Edward's life and the anger at Susan Lee's co-worker, I realized I could barge into a trap. Did they know I dispatched their faithful killing machine? Or were they luring me by using Edward as bait? It wouldn't be so different from what I had done with Claudette.

The ghosts taunted me now. Thousands of them filled the street, making it almost difficult to see the real world. Layered one on top of the other, they were too compact to make out individual features. I wanted to scream at them, forcing them out of my path. When I needed them earlier, they deserted me, and now they haphazardly got in my way.

I allowed them to stay, scared that if I let the flame dwindle in my palm, I wouldn't be able to call them again. I don't know why, but somebody capable of controlling a psychotic killer had me more worried than the killer himself. At least a man with a blade slitting the throats of mentalists was easy to understand. Whoever controlled them had a more meticulous mind.

I walked past the street leading to the front door and crept into the alley behind the row of expensive townhomes. A tall brick wall separated the rear courtyard from the alley. Unlike the adjacent houses, the doctor's house had wrought iron spears at the top, preventing any would-be cat burglar from jumping over. Between that and the massive lock on the gate opening into the yard, I would have to find another way in.

I'm not sure why it came to mind, but the green demon from my vision would have been able to fly over the wall. If she couldn't, the muscles in her arms would be large enough, she could have torn the gate off its hinges. I didn't have wings or strength, and unless a mentalist had the ability to levitate, I'd need another solution.

The ghosts in the alley were a fraction of those on the street. I watched as several reached up the wall, doing something to a loose brick near the next neighbor's gate. A quick investigation revealed the grout around the rock had long since vanished and behind it, a spare key. That got me into the neighbor's courtyard. It was at least a step closer.

In the middle of lush greenery, a water fountain stood as tall as myself. The rain falling made little kerplunk sounds in the basin. There were lovely benches for two on either side, with dozens of rose bushes creating a chest-high maze. Vines climbing the wall next to the doctor's house interested me the most.

I followed the pavers to a rose garden past its peak bloom. Behind it, ivy snaked in and out of a trellis. I found my way in. I might not fly or be able to crush a metal gate, but I managed. After the first few rungs, I knew I'd be spending time lifting weights at the gym. I could take a hit and move quickly, but I had never really been in shape. Frank and I would be talking tomorrow.

I reached the top of the wall, straddling it, lying low to make sure I wouldn't be seen. The house was some place I'd love to live, not that I could afford the mortgage. There was no fountain below, which made their yard feel modest by comparison, but it had more greenery than my entire block.

White blinds were drawn tight, but a faint glimmer on the inside cast a shadow on the fabric. I froze as the shadow moved. One person: large, broad shoulders. I couldn't recall the doctor's physique enough to remember if he fit the description. Whether or not he did, I had to go.

The light turned off, leaving the house wrapped in shadow. This was a trap, but without a small garrison of police officers, I was Edward's only hope.

I slid down the wall, dropping the last foot. I hissed at the pain from my—everything. Kneeling down on the grass, I waited to see if there was movement. Any sound hid behind a crack of thunder. I feared a flash of lightning would give away my position.

Up to this point, I acted, moving forward. A pang of fear broke through my armor and continued to stab at my chest. I didn't know if I could win another fight. For a moment, I considered going for reinforcements, calling Frank, or even the police. I had no idea how much time Edward had left. I decided to push on.

The ghosts in the garden were few and far between, and those that remained had started to fade. If the killer could detect mentalists, was there a way one could shut off their abilities? The only man who might be able to answer that was hidden somewhere in this house.

I crept up the stairs on my hands and feet, staying low to the ground. The porch ran the width of the building. It had been built for entertaining. The tall windows surrounded the ballroom. There had been dancing and merriment a week before, and now, without the music or laughter, there was an air of horror surrounding the place.

The double French doors were slightly ajar, the lock scraped and broken. Why would the killer have to break in if the doctor was his master? A single clue shook my conspiracy theory. Perhaps the killer wasn't controlled by the doctor. Maybe they were in cahoots and this was how loose ends were corrected.

I eased the door open and found one of the massive velvet drapes blocking the entrance. I carefully slid inside, using the fabric to dry the water from my hands. Peaking around the curtains, it was hard to see. The thick drapes and lack of wall sconces left the room almost pitch black.

A moan sounded from somewhere in the room. It was Edward. He was alive. *Edward, are you okay?* I screamed the thoughts in my head. I didn't know if he could hear them or not.

"Eleanor," the voice was raspy, dried to the point where I wasn't entirely sure it came from Edward.

A crack of lightning penetrated the thick curtains, giving a slight glow to the room. I found Edward tied to one of the chairs in the center of the dance floor. His head hung to the side, with his arms bound behind his back. This was a problem to solve another time. I didn't need to know who the killer worked for or his association to the doctor. I simply needed to rescue Edward and flee.

I waited until another bit of lightning filled the room. While the thunder shook the sky, I scanned the room, looking for anybody who might be hiding amongst the bar or dinner tables. The area for the band and the seating for patrons were empty. I ran for it.

My boots squeaked across the floor as I crossed the dance floor. I slipped and slid as I ran, the water pouring off my trousers as I made my way to Edward.

"Edward," I whispered, "are you okay?"

I scooted behind him, following his arms to the ropes binding his wrists. I didn't have a knife to cut him free. If we made it out of here, I'd make sure I always carried a knife. I let my fingers follow the rope, trying to visualize how it had been tied. Finding a loose end, I tried shimmying it back through the complex knot.

I froze. I couldn't be sure, the rain made it difficult to feel out the room, but I swore I heard footsteps. Letting go of the rope, I stood slowly. Reaching into my jacket pocket, I pulled out the brass knuckles and slid the fingers of my right hand into the tiny circles. My palm ached, well worn from my earlier fight.

"I know it's you," I whispered into the emptiness.

"Uh," Edward moaned. His head leaned back, bumping into my stomach. I couldn't make out his face, but I imagined he smiled, thankful I came to save him.

"Eleanor," even my name sounded garbled.

"I'm here."

"Two," he said. I couldn't hear the whole sentence. He sounded parched, in desperate need of water. Before he could speak again, lightning struck nearby. Even the thick velvet curtains couldn't keep out the flash of white light.

"Two killers," Edward gasped.

The twisted smile was pulled taut on his face. Several teeth were missing, ones I had knocked out of his jaw. Gaping in the jacket, a hole where Claudette had shot him. The killer held a razor against his cheek, pressing down on the skin hard enough a line of red had formed.

It all fell into place.

"Dammit."

Chapter Thirty

Darkness. My memory attempted to fill in the gaps. I braced my foot on the back of Edward's chair and kicked with all my might. The scream forced its way out of my mouth as he skid along the floor and tumbled with a thud. It wasn't far, but enough that he wasn't between the killer and me.

I raised my fists, making sure my hands protected my face. It might be the one time I didn't need a reminder from Frank. My shoes squeaked, and I froze. I could swear the shadows moved, and I turned, trying to follow. He moved without making a sound, far more comfortable with the darkness than me.

Movement to my right forced me to turn. Metal ground against metal as the blade dragged across my forearm. I didn't have time to reflect on Emma Jean's uncanny ability to weave metallic strips into the jacket. I punched a wide sweeping blow. Nothing. I pulled my fists back to my head, hoping I could land a single hit. If I could strike him once, I could follow it with a second.

It happened quickly—the blade swiping at my side. It caught enough skin that I hissed, but the metal boning prevented it from being a killing blow. Each victim had been killed in an identical manner, head drawn back with a slit across the throat. Something had changed. This wasn't about a quick kill. He baited me, torturing me with a thousand cuts. He turned from efficient to sadistic. I didn't like the change.

I took a chance. Throwing my elbow back, I touched something just out of reach. Swinging about, I used my fist like a club. I hit something, fabric, perhaps an arm. I put all my weight on my bad leg and screamed. Kicking, I landed the heel of my foot into flesh, knocking it away. I could hear it smack against the floor.

I bolted in the opposite direction. My boots didn't slip, but they made a noise. I nearly tripped, my toe kicking against something on the floor. They stopped, no more squeaking. I stood on the carpet where the round dinner tables had been placed. Continuing, I bumped a chair with my injured leg. I bit back a yelp, trying to hide in the silence like the killer.

Every step, I feared I'd open my eyes, and there would be that smile, inches from my face. I held one hand in front of me, feeling the table as I moved through the room. Paranoia set in, and I convinced myself there were more faces hovering just out of reach.

I tried holding my breath, listening for motion. Nicholas claimed his hearing became more acute after he lost his sight. I'd call him a liar. The only sound in the ballroom came from billowing winds and my heartbeat. Despite fear rolling off me like the smell of a bad whiskey, the ghosts refused to show. I didn't have a chance to question the accuracy of the vision depicting my death. It'd be ironic, my first time changing the future due to a premature demise.

Light flashed outside, lighting up the room. I spun about, looking for the killer. The exit to the front of the estate, the bar, even Edward on the dance floor. Nowhere did I see a man preparing to kill. The thunder boomed, and I made a run for the study.

I hadn't gone ten steps when I hit somebody. Bracing myself with my forearms protecting my face, I fell. We landed with a thud, me on top of the other person. I crawled as fast as I could. It grabbed at my legs, catching my ankle. I screamed. Panicked. I rolled over. With my other foot, I slammed into flesh. It didn't matter what; it let go.

On my hands and knees, I crawled until I could get to my feet and hobble away. If I could get a moment to breathe, to focus, the ghosts would appear. Once they appeared, the darkness wouldn't matter. I never thought it would happen, but I needed them. Without their predictions, I was going to die.

The wall, the hip-high chair rail, I followed them. They vanished into an opening, the doorway that led to the front of the house. My fingers stayed in contact with the wallpaper. Every now and then, they grazed a door frame, but I had no idea what might be behind each door. The only doors that mattered were the study and the exit. For a moment, I contemplated running out the front and standing in the street, hoping to lure the killer out. No, in the study, there'd only be one entrance and I was certain I could find a weapon.

I slowed as a light came from the small corridor leading to the study. Inside, something illuminated the room. It wasn't bright, but it'd be enough to level the playing field. I stood a chance. Out here in the darkness, the shadows could kill me at any moment.

Moving quickly, I reached the door and slipped inside. Shutting it quietly behind me, I found a roaring fire. Dr. Butler's face glistened in the light. The man's head leaned to one side as if he had dozed off while reading a good book. I didn't trust him any more than I did the killer.

"Sir," I whispered. Nothing.

I inched closer, careful to keep checking over my shoulder to make sure the doors didn't burst open. The sheen on his face didn't come from sweat. Blood speckled his face and clothes. It took another two steps before I realized he had a hole in his chest. Somebody had shot him. Unless the man with the razor blade changed his methods, there was another killer.

There was no need to check his pulse. Even if he had been alive, nothing I could do would prevent him from dying. Instead, my eyes followed the direction of the hole and found across the rug in an identical chair, a woman holding a gun. The man's wife. She remained frozen, so still that when she blinked, I nearly had a heart attack.

"Hello?"

It was difficult to hear with the crackling of the fire, but her lips moved. "He made me do it."

"Do what? Did he hurt you?" If the doctor had been a corrupt man, it proved that my judgment of character needed a fine-tuning.

"Our son…" Her eyes drifted upward, connecting with mine.

"There's a killer out there, we need to go." When I reached for her, she lifted the gun. It didn't quite point at me, but it was close enough that I stopped approaching.

"He sacrificed our son," she mumbled, "for this." Her arms gestured to the room. The photographs had depicted a cheerful couple and once their son appeared the joy seemed to fade. Did Mrs. Butler finally snap and kill her husband for something that happened years ago?

"We'll deal with that later. But there's a killer here. The man in the bomber jacket—"

"You met him?" Her voice perked up at the mention of a killer. Something was—

"He's your son?" She didn't mean they had killed her son, just his personality. If he was indeed her child, then I had to worry. I wanted her son dead, and she had a gun. The last person to do harm to her kid was bleeding in the chair.

"Why is he killing people?"

"Mentalists?" Slowly, she stood from the chair, making me take a step back. I bumped into an open globe. Tempting me, it held a nearly full decanter of whiskey. I resisted the urge. "Mentalists are what made him this way. He was such a sweet boy. They took that from him, and for what?" Her voice grew louder, and I suspected this festering wound was going to get worse.

"I'm so sorry." I wasn't, but I didn't want a bullet between my eyes.

"He sold our baby to the Society for money." She spat on the floor.

"The Society?"

He's coming. Edward's voice held a note of urgency mixed with pain. Even tied up in a chair, being a telepath meant he was not restrained by the body. For once, the gift was a blessing.

"Give me the gun."

She raised the weapon. The sneer on her face and the movement of her other hand to steady it made it clear she wouldn't relinquish it. I snatched the bottle of whiskey and hurled it. She shielded her eyes as the glass struck the fireplace and a ball of flame erupted outward.

I lunged and grabbed her wrist. She couldn't wiggle free from my grip. I slammed my forehead against her face, striking her nose. Refusing to let go of the gun, I hooked my foot behind her leg and shoved with my shoulder. On the way down, she kicked my leg. I screamed. The gun fell out of sight, but she remained down.

"Good Lord..."

"God turns a blind eye on us."

With a boot to the gut, she curled into a ball. "Shut up." I couldn't kill her, at least I wouldn't kill her. She might have been the reason the doctor was dead, but that was for the police to sort out. The serial killer, however, he needed a knife to the chest.

Bits of fire spread to the carpet, and I wondered if it was enough to burn down the entire building. Stomping on them, I decided I couldn't let their neighbors fall victim to this search-and-rescue gone wrong. The gun had slid somewhere along the floor, and I didn't want to be on my hands and knees when the doors burst open. Then I saw my weapon.

The black poker had ample weight to make it dangerous, but light enough I could swing with some amount of control.

A bit of the whiskey bottled remained intact on the hearth of the fireplace, the liquid in the chunk of glass burning shades of blue. Beautiful, serene, and reminiscent of the match stick I used to conjure the ghosts.

Fire begot fire and the match in my head ignited.

Chapter Thirty-One

I clutched the poker with both hands, standing at the door. The specter of Mrs. Butler seemed content to stay on the floor for the next few minutes, but not the killer. His ghost flung open the door and charged in, trying to pin me to a corner. In my head, I'd wait for the moment he barreled into the room, and with a single swipe, I'd crack his skull hard enough to end the fight.

I reminded myself, this is not where I died. The ghosts don't lie. The ghosts don't lie. The ghosts—

The door flung inward. Flickering light from the fireplace made the shadows stretch across his face like long, slender fingers. One of the black digits appeared to pull the edges of the smile further. His teeth shimmered, fueling this nightmare. I reminded myself that he was nothing more than a man with a razor. A very mortal man.

He rushed forward, the blade prepared to drag across my torso. I swung the poker like a baseball bat. Without space to wind up, he managed to block the blow. Bone snapped. His lunge shifted, and he bounced off the wall, trying to brace himself—the books on the shelf scattered along the floor.

I didn't dare swing again. I got in front of him and shoved the poker forward. He managed to push it high, but it connected with his shoulder. I thrust, forcing him backward. Leaning into it, I used my bodyweight to force the man from the room. Into the hall we went until I had him pinned against the wall. My throat burned as I unleashed an ear pitching scream, trying to force the metal through his body.

I watched as his ghost dropped the blade. Reaching up, he grabbed the metal shaft and pulled it free as if I were a minor inconvenience. It took a moment before I realized I could see the man. Even with the light from the study, we stood in a near pitch-black hall. His actual hand dropped the blade and reached for the poker. Letting go, I shoved him to the side.

I hobbled toward the darkness of the ballroom. I had a plan.

Pain seared up my leg, not even the adrenaline eased the nerves shouting for me to stop. With a scuffle not far behind me and the sound of the poker being tossed against a wall, I kept moving. My hand touched the door, moving along, finding my way back to the ballroom. I had to get away from the light, and reach an open space in the darkness. If he caught me with my back turned, he'd kill me. My throat tightened at the thought of the blade sliding through my skin.

There was no point in hiding the sound, my feet on the carpet, my hand smacking the drywall, my panting. The moment I crossed the threshold to the ballroom, the sound changed. The emptiness swallowed my breathing. I pushed forward, moving along the rug to a space adjacent to the dinner tables. I didn't dare step onto the dance floor, not with water dripping from my clothes.

The flame had nearly extinguished. My determination and stubbornness did nothing to coax it back to life. Each time I tried, it threatened to vanish. I let the fear take hold, the worry that if I died here tonight, it proved a malleable future. If the killer managed to sink the blade into my flesh, it'd only be a matter of time before he butchered Edward. Each mentalist they slaughtered could have been a teacher, a companion, a friend. That *thing* robbed me of the chance to learn from those like me. Fear turned to rage.

The flame feasted on the anger until it filled my hands.

Edward's ghost lay on the floor on the other side of the dance floor. The white of the specter shone through the darkness. I couldn't see Edward himself, but I didn't need to. The darkness welcomed the ghosts.

I spun about on my good leg and watched the ghost of the killer in the doorway. If he could sense mentalists, he could probably see me just the same. I didn't need an advantage. I needed a level playing field. Raising my hands, I clenched my fists. My muscles tightened as the adrenaline gave way to pure unbridled rage.

The blade in the ghost's hand flipped open. Was it the same one that killed nearly a dozen New York mentalists? Did it still have their blood on the edge? My nails bit into my palms as I dwelled on those extinguished before their time.

The killer had at least a hundred ghosts, each a fraction of a second in front of the next. He'd charge, his arm tucked in tight to make a fast cut to my torso. I forced myself to focus on the ghost only a second ahead of its owner. He ran toward me, the present catching up to the future.

I swung my left arm down, smacking against his forearm and blocking the blade. My right fist jabbed hard at his nose, crushing the bone under my knuckles. Unlike opponents in the ring, he didn't stagger or stumble backward. He pulled the blade back quickly, slicing through the fabric of the coat and striking one of the flimsy metal rods inside.

Time froze. A series of ghosts swung again, this time going for my neck. Frank would yell at me for what I attempted next. As time resumed, I reached out, guiding the killer's arm. Ducking under the blade, I pushed his arm. He turned enough that I put all my weight on my bad leg and kicked. Striking him in the hip, he fell and tumbled along the carpet.

With an almost supernatural speed, he crawled to his feet. I moved toward the tables until I bumped against one. For whatever reason, the inanimate objects in the room didn't have their own ghosts. I grabbed one of the wooden chairs.

The killer moved too fast to prepare a full swing. The chair smashed against his side, knocking him onto a table. I held onto the back, and next time he darted at me, I stepped in close. I smashed the shield against his face. Bringing up my foot, I drove it into his knee. The crack of bone brought a smile to my face even as the weapon

197

dragged along my stomach. Emma Jean's handiwork continued to hold.

I slammed the back of the chair against his hand. The knife fell somewhere along the carpet, its ghost vanishing as it disconnected from his body. I took too long thinking about the weapon, giving him the chance to reach for my neck with his other hand. I swatted, trying to keep him from latching onto me. My foot caught as I tried to turn.

I landed with a thud. He hovered above me. I tried to push away, but he fell, landing with his head just above my stomach. Kicking and squirming, I couldn't get free. The killer's bodyweight pinned me down. He pushed himself forward, hand resting on the wound in my leg.

I screamed. Terror set in as I watched the ghost of the man inch his way up my body. Despite being a white translucent figure, the blood rolling from his nose and down his lip made him more terrifying. Pushing off with one hand, I tried to roll my weight so I could flip over, but he held my hips, forcing me back into place.

Fear. Unable to get away, I struggled. If I was going to die, I wouldn't make it easy.

"Get off me!"

The ghosts flashed out of sequence. I couldn't tell which came first. I didn't have time to think. One ghost hovered inches from my face, the smile turning into a sadistic snarl. I didn't die here. I couldn't die. He grabbed onto my shoulder, dragging himself along my body. I flailed, reaching, praying I found his blade or a piece of the chair.

His weight pinned my legs and then my torso. The ghost hovering over my face stopped being the future. The heat of his breath spread across my neck. He straddled my hips, one hand pressing against the center of my throat. I kicked my legs, hoping to buck him to the side, but he refused to relent. His fingernails dug into my flesh as he tightened his grip.

There were only seconds before I went unconscious. He used his weight to press down, cutting off my windpipe. I couldn't pull his hand free. I punched at the inside of his elbow, forcing his arm to bend. The scent of the killer's breath was close enough I winced. The putrid smell almost forced me to turn away from his face.

Nails dragged across his face, searching for anything to damage. I attempted to jab at his throat but couldn't get enough leverage to do more than clumsily slap him. I tried to suck in air but found it impossible.

Grabbing the sides of his head, I tried to push him to the side. My hand slid across his face, unable to—

I plunged my right thumb into his eye socket. My left followed suit. I pushed, burrowing as deep as his skull allowed. He only let go of my throat to knock my arms to the side. It was enough to cough and suck in a much-needed breath. With him sitting further back, I jabbed again at his throat, this time the tips of my fingers jammed against his Adam's apple.

"Die," I screamed.

I couldn't stay on the ground. If he pinned me again, I'd be— I needed to get up. Grabbing onto the bomber jacket, I pull myself upright. My forehead smashed against his nose. His weight shifted, and I rolled as hard as I could. We turned to our side.

I straddled him.

As I threw my weight down on the killer to hold him in place, my fingers touched the wood from the back of the chair. He tried to blindly grab my arms. Smacking them away, I smashed the wood against his face, once, twice, a third time. It shattered in my hand, leaving a long slender stake.

I could see his ghost as the wood punctured his neck. Presently, he clawed at my face. But not even he could stop the future from happening. It was even more terrifying when the lights in the ballroom flashed to life. Gaping holes for eyes and bleeding gashes was horrific.

The smile persisted.

"Die."

I crammed the piece of wood into his neck. His body convulsed, refusing to accept death. I shocked myself when I pulled the wood free and slammed it in again. With a jerk of the wrists, the stake spun as blood bubbled from the wound.

The jerking body tensed one last time. The killer's muscles

relaxed. I needed to find Edward and make sure he was okay. Once I got him untied, we'd get out of this madhouse. At least the killers were dead, it was progress.

It was over.

Until a wailing filled the air, and something smashed into the side of my body.

Chapter Thirty-Two

I woke to weeping.

Everything hurt. The cut, the bruising on my ribs, and I could still feel the killer's hand on my throat. I reached the extreme of what my body could tolerate. Blinking seemed to be the only thing that didn't threaten to empty the contents of my stomach.

"My poor baby," Mrs. Butler cooed. The woman cradled the son I murdered. Bile rose in my throat as she carefully pulled the wood from his body.

"You killed him," she hissed at me. She lifted him, scooting closer so he could sit half propped in her lap. It took a moment before I realized the way she caressed his forehead was as if she moved the hair from his eyes. The woman had clearly lost her mind.

"I should never have let him give you away."

"To the Society?" I asked. I needed answers. Why were mentalists being hunted. Whether or not she decided to kill me, I couldn't die with this uncertainty hanging over my head.

"You did this to him!" she screamed. The ear-piercing wail was loud enough to wake the dead. "He should have killed you first."

"Why mentalists?"

She reached along the carpet and raised the gun. With only a few feet separating us, I was certain she'd land a bullet in the center of my face.

"Why kill mentalists?"

"You work for them, don't you? You're just like them, a killer."

Her hand shook as she pulled back the hammer. The wobble of the barrel only meant it'd land somewhere between my eye and my chin. A face shot still meant death.

"Who is the Society? Why did they—"

She lifted her hand. Bang. It flew harmlessly overhead. Four more shots. The grieving mother drew back the hammer again, this time steadying herself as she returned to my face.

"Who are they?"

"Don't treat me like a fool. They…"

Her eyes remained fixated on me, but quickly glossed over. I suddenly felt as if she wasn't seeing me at all, or perhaps staring through me.

"Tell me!"

My words fell on deaf ears. Slowly, she bent her arm, the gun no longer pointing at my face. Her head tipped back, and the barrel pressed into the space under the jaw. It took a moment before I realized she wasn't acting of her own accord.

"Edward," I screamed, "stop it. We need—"

The shot fired, and I froze. Her hand fell, the gun dropping onto the dead killer. A moment later she slouched down, her upper body draping over her dead son. It only seemed fitting that the two clung to one another as their souls vacated their bodies.

Are you okay?

Dealing with a killer had made me forget our earlier tiff. I wanted nothing more than to hobble my way over to the man and wrap my arms around him.

We won. I couldn't muster the ecstatic victory cheer I wanted. The throbbing in my leg moved in time with my heart. I'd celebrate after we were far from here, away from the grime and blood.

You came for me. I could hear the surprise in his voice. The disbelief grew from a place of hurt and rejection. Did he believe I'd leave him to be carved up by a killer?

"Thank you."

Edward stood over me rubbing the burns along his wrists. His head blocked out the light from a chandelier creating a halo that made him appear angelic. When push came to shove, we saved one another tonight.

"I don't know if I can walk," I admitted.

"Put your weight on me." He reached down, lifting from underneath my armpits. "The neighbors probably heard the gunshots. We need to leave before the police show."

When I got upright, he slid my arm around his neck. We didn't so much walk by side as him lifting me to my feet.

"We won," I repeated.

"You won," he said.

He carried me toward the rear doors. Yes, I did in fact win.

THIRTY-THREE

Epilogue

Veterans are an odd lot. They've been trained to kill, to endure the worst humankind has to offer. To see them on the street would set off alarms, their scars, gruff manner, and steely gazes burrowing a hole through your head. The only thing more frightening than a vet was the determination and optimism of Susan Lee.

I pushed a newly delivered bin of bandages through the back doors of the gym. The sea of white fabric had been dumped inside, the raw material that might someday save a serviceman overseas. Before we could ship them from New York to France, they needed to be rolled and counted. In just a few short weeks, we had managed just shy of ten thousand bandages, an impressive number to anybody other than my roommate.

"Is that it?" She had a skip in her step as she approached.

Frank's gym, a place to hone the body and excise demons through physical labor, now had developed an altruistic side project.

"The driver said he'd have more next week."

Her brow furrowed, and it was obvious as she snagged the bin that she was not happy.

I joined her at the long row of tables covered in rolls of bandages. For such a prim and proper woman, she demonstrated a work ethic that defied reason. If the vets in the gym weren't pulling their weight, she'd set eyes upon them and invoke the wrath of God.

"You know," Michael said, "I'm starting to think bandages aren't the answer. Why not send Susan Lee to Germany? I bet she'd have Hitler begging for mercy in no time."

I snorted. "Why would you be so cruel?"

"Susan Lee," Frank yelled from a nearby table. "I need help."

The three of us turned to see Frank with knitting needles, holding up what should have been a sock. Bandage rolling had been going exceptionally well. I could not say the same for teaching veterans how to knit.

"What would they do without me?"

I held my hand up to Michael, halting his sarcasm. "You do not want her lecturing you. You'd wish you were overseas fighting."

Her makeshift volunteer outpost would continue for another hour. Then she'd have to go work at the hospital and the gym would return to normal. I was happy to see a delightful balance between the people I cared for.

Frank and Susan Lee bickered as she shook her head at his efforts. She was an excellent teacher, Frank, however, was anything but an exemplary student. I envied her patience, something I hoped would someday rub off on me.

"Susan Lee," I shouted, "I have to step out for a few. Leave everything out and I'll make sure the bandages get delivered."

She gave me a thumbs-up before smacking Frank on the hand. Michael was right. If we could bottle that woman's energy and ship it overseas, the war would be won and world peace would erupt across the globe.

Outside, it was hard to imagine we were in the midst of turmoil. A cool breeze came off the harbor, and the sun held fast in the sky. With news of the killers being slain, the streets returned to normal. Women walked with their children to shops and stoops became areas where folks congregated to talk about the war. It wasn't perfect, but it was a step in the right direction. It was even more rewarding seeing the streets free of unwanted ghosts.

I ventured to the park, my head held high, meeting the curious gazes of women walking by. I remained an oddity, a woman not quite fitting into the standards of beauty or fashion. For the first time since childhood, I embraced my idiosyncrasies.

Eventually Edward would be along, hopefully supplying a cherry Penny Sundae. Despite the fact he had been abducted and tied up; I was covered in bruises. Thankfully the pain had subsided and most of the bruises faded. I still think he owed me shaved ice. In our relationship, he'd have to settle for being the damsel while I was the knight in shining armor. It seemed fitting.

For the first days, he had been calm, spending his time in bed healing. We laid there talking about what we remembered about our families and our favorite books. Despite not taking nearly the beating I did, I applied Claudette's salve to his wrists like a good girlfriend. I thought, or at least I hoped, he'd come away a changed man. But the anger lingered, and I worried it took up permanent residence in his. I hoped that he managed to find redemption and calm his feelings of superiority. I'm sure we'd discuss it as we savored the beautiful day.

I walked through the park as I thought of the crooked smirk plastered on his face. I dismissed the idea each time Susan Lee brought it up, but I could see myself loving him. He might not be perfect, but I was firmly aware that I had my own broken bits. I hoped we could set our differences aside and we'd find a way to mend the other. Afterall, we were a precog and a telepath, weirder things were known to happen.

I occupied my usual bench at the park. A month ago, I came here to hide away from the world, to avoid people and their ghosts. Now, it felt like a distant memory, a younger version of myself slipping into the past. With a slight nudge, the imaginary flame sprung to life, and the ghosts appeared. A woman guided her son along, shooing away the pigeons. Just as quickly, the flame vanished, and so did the ghosts.

"I'm finally in control." The words were foreign, a sensation I never expected to experience in my lifetime. Light bathed the park in a warmth that had been absent over the past week, and something about the world felt right. I couldn't be sure if it was this growing sense of empowerment or that I was a tiny part of why people enjoyed the day. But it was there, a seedling nurtured by the intensity of the sun.

"Eleanor," The owner of the voice had approached me from behind, without making a sound in the grass. I casually bent over as if I was adjusting the buckle on my right boot. The world might feel right, but I had learned my lesson. My hand slid inside the soft leather and tightened around the hilt of a rifle bayonet.

"I mean you no harm, Ms. Bouvier."

Knowing my first name made him creepy. Knowing my last made him dangerous. His assurance loosened the tension in my arm and I reclined, believing his words. The calm washed over my body.

He stepped around the bench, a portly fellow in a three-piece suit that hugged him a bit too tightly around the mid-section. He sat with me a moment before he twirled the length of his mustache, a nervous habit I wasn't sure he was aware of.

"It's a beautiful day," I said.

"It would be if it didn't come with such bad tidings."

The jolliness of his face faded, replaced by a serious expression that bordered on sadness. He stopped fiddling with his facial hair and rested his hands together in his lap. I had a sudden urge to offer the man a hug, to help ward off whatever grief nipped at the edge of his thoughts.

"They're coming, Eleanor," he said softly. "For you."

- The End -

Continue the Adventure

For More Children of Nostradamus Visit
www.childrenofnostradamus.com